IF I LOVED YOU

IF I LOVED YOU

THE CABIN OF LOVE & MAGIC: BOOK 1

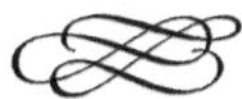

JOANNE PENCE

QUAIL HILL PUBLISHING

Quail Hill Publishing

PO Box 64

Eagle, ID 83616

Visit our website at www.quailhillpublishing.net

First Quail Hill Publishing E-book: January 2021

First Quail Hill Publishing Print Book: January 2021

ISBN: 978-1-949566-35-2

IF I LOVED YOU

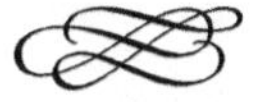

*This trilogy about the magic of love is for David,
forever in my heart.*

CHAPTER 1

Carly Fullerton unlocked the cabin's front door. As she stepped into the entry hall, everything seemed smaller and older than she remembered. Sixteen years had passed since she was last there.

As a child, she'd been convinced that the cabin was haunted and maybe even held a touch of magic. Of course, there was nothing magical or scary about the old place. It was simply a cabin built in the 1890s in a remote Idaho valley and handed down through her family from generation to generation. The original building had been no more than a square built of logs. Over the years, relatives had remodeled and added to it so that it now stood two stories tall.

The knotty pine walls had darkened with age, but shimmered in the light that shone through the window beside the door. An elk-horn lantern hung overhead. The rough-hewn wooden staircase to the far right of the entry hall led up to three bedrooms and one bathroom. Carly stood a moment remembering how, as a child, she often wished she could live there year round.

Of course, it never happened. Not only did her parents

develop "irreconcilable differences" when Carly was only five years old, but her mother would never have agreed to live in a place where it snowed in winter.

Carly pushed aside such memories and continued straight ahead to what was once called the parlor.

Her jaw dropped. Was this really the cabin she'd visited all those years before? The change was remarkable.

Last year, her mother, Roxanne Donnelly, had died from a sudden heart attack, leaving the cabin to her three daughters, Carly Fullerton, Julia Perrin, and Mallory Conway. The women had different fathers, all were unmarried, and didn't resemble each other at all. Julia, the eldest, was small and blond; Mallory, the youngest, had black hair and a sleek, model's figure; while middle-child Carly was tall, with red hair, and a comfortably curvaceous build.

Carly's immediate thought had been that the three should sell the cabin and each take their share of the money—money Carly desperately needed. But her sisters didn't agree. Julia was adamant that the cabin was part of their family history, and Mallory apparently didn't want to argue with her oldest sister. Carly "in the middle" went along with them, as usual.

At the time she never expected she'd turn to the cabin as a refuge. But that was exactly what she was now doing.

But before the sisters could do anything with the cabin, they needed to be practical. Because their mother had neglected it for years, they had to use the little money they'd inherited from her to make it habitable again. Julia had volunteered to oversee the project. She took down the walls separating the kitchen, dining room and parlor to make an open, airy great room, updated the kitchen, and added French doors out to the back porch.

"Julia, you astound me!" Carly said with a laugh, parroting a line often said in the Sherlock Holmes mysteries she loved.

The way the cabin now looked, Carly understood why Julia

had mentioned the possibility of someday turning it into a vacation rental. People might actually want to spend time here, as long as they didn't mind being so isolated.

And didn't hear stories of the ghosts that haunted it.

The many ghost stories Carly had heard about the cabin and the creepy things she and her sisters had sworn went bump in the night came back to her now. She couldn't help but shiver.

She didn't believe in ghosts or enchantment or magic. But still…

Her gaze shot to the portrait over the fireplace of Elijah Donnelly, who was her mother's great-great uncle. The story was that Elijah had built the cabin for his bride, but they both died at a young age. The son, Lucas, was said to have painted his father's portrait. It showed a handsome young man with blond hair parted just off center and slicked down. His white shirt collar stood high against his neck, and a gray and white striped tie formed a full Windsor knot. His charcoal gray jacket had narrow, notched lapels with a white carnation pinned to one of them. The jacket lay unbuttoned to show a light gray vest.

But how, the people in the area wondered, did Lucas know what his father looked like? After all, he had been an infant when Elijah died—Lucas was raised by his aunt—and no other portraits or photographs of Elijah existed. Did Lucas make-up his father's appearance, or did he—in some mysterious way—actually know how he'd looked? And, most of all, were Elijah's eyes really the strange violet shade Lucas had painted them?

Those eyes. Even now, they filled Carly with the same uneasiness they had given her as a child. They intrigued and mystified her, and she couldn't shake the eerie sensation that Elijah was staring at her, trying to tell her something just beyond her ability to grasp.

Rubbing the goosebumps that rose on her arms, she turned away from the portrait and hurried out to her car to unload it and settle in. She realized she'd never before been all alone in the cabin and thinking about scary ghost stories was not the way to get a sorely needed rest.

"Stop being so silly," she ordered herself.

After she finished putting away the few supplies and water she had brought from home, she carried her suitcase upstairs to the biggest and brightest bedroom, the one called the "river view room," that she had always wanted to sleep in. She would unpack later. Right now, all she wanted to do was stand at the window and gaze out at the river and the lush greenery and patches of wildflowers surrounding it, while listening to the songs of birds as they flitted from tree to tree.

This was what she desperately needed. Time to think. Time to plan. Here. Alone.

Unless the cabin really was haunted.

She grinned at that thought, but then jumped when she heard a creak on the stairs.

She dashed out of the room, looked up and down the hallway, and went to the stairwell. She saw no one, nothing. Obviously, her imagination was at work. Old buildings creak.

If she'd been at home, she never would have noticed such a minuscule sound. In San Francisco, the din from people, cars, buses, cable cars, and an occasional foghorn was constant. Here, however, she heard the quiet.

Back downstairs, she placed her laptop on the kitchen island, opened it to log onto Wi-Fi, and discovered there was none. Not surprising, she guessed, considering the remoteness of the cabin.

She pulled out her cell phone and saw that it had only one bar. And that flickered to nothing every few seconds.

Good. No one could call, text or email her to complain about anything. She could be left alone to think. But what if there was an emergency?

Her gaze went to the old black dial telephone sitting on an

antique table at the foot of the stairs. Maybe it wasn't for decoration only. Was it possible?

Under the watchful gaze of Elijah Donnelly, she hurried to the entryway and lifted the phone's large receiver. Much to her relief, a dial tone hummed. Her sister had thought of everything. *Thank you, Julia.*

She sauntered back into the kitchen again, steadfastly repeating to herself that everything would be fine. Just fine. The one thing that would make it better was a cup of coffee. When at work, she practically lived on the stuff and would take it intravenously if she could.

From the refrigerator, she pulled out the container of French roast she'd brought, opened the bag and inhaled its scent. She smiled—until she realized after searching the cabinets that there wasn't a drip coffee maker or even an old percolator in sight, only one of the newer coffee machines that needed pods, something she was lacking. So much for her immediate coffee fix.

Thankfully, she wasn't all that far from town. She grabbed her handbag and headed out the door. She could drive to the Old West town of Crouch in minutes and hit the grocery store for coffee pods, food, and a few supplies. Then, back at the cabin, she would brew a cup, and take it out to the back porch to enjoy the peace, quiet, and blessed solitude it offered.

Take that, ghosts!

Alex Townson pulled into the driveway of the YourB&B cabin he had rented for the month. It looked decent enough on the outside. He hoped he could say the same about the inside. No matter what, he was relieved to finally be here. The drive from the streets of Boston to the mountains of Idaho had been long. Beyond long.

A tall, rangy man, with dark brown hair and green eyes, his

thirty-seven years had given him a solemn, serious countenance. Now, he got out of his Mercedes SUV and had just clicked the latch on its back door when his black Newfoundland, Hitchcock, named after Alex's favorite thriller-suspense movie director, pushed it open with his nose and leaped out. He bounded around the driveway, as much as a 160-pound dog could bound, and sniffed the trees and vegetation. Hitch, as he was called, was the reason Alex had made this a road trip.

Perhaps he was crazy, but no way would he let his dog fly in a cargo hold for hours. Hitchcock was more than a pet to him, and lately he'd come to the painful realization that Hitchcock just might be his only true friend.

What did that say about the way he'd lived his life?

As he waited for Hitchcock to finish sniffing the cabin's front yard and marking half the trees in the area, he breathed deeply. No cars. No people. The chirping of birds and the faint ripple of water over rocks from the nearby river were music to ears used to far harsher sounds. Years had passed since he'd last been in clean mountain air. He had almost forgotten what it smelled like.

Around him, he saw no sign at all of human activity, and for the first time in weeks, maybe months, he felt a glimmer of hope that he might find some contentment. In that moment, a hint of a smile touched the firm, straight line of his mouth and softened the hard contours of his face.

He walked up to the garage door, used the code he had been sent to open it, and then drove the Mercedes inside. An interior door led from the garage into the house. He quickly unloaded the SUV, carrying his suitcase, laptop, food he'd picked up at the last gas station he'd stopped at, plus Hitchcock's hefty sack of dog food into the cabin.

The cabin was larger than he'd expected, and older, but it suited his purposes well enough. Someone's laptop sat on the kitchen island, and he found bottled water and condiments in the refrigerator. He guessed they belonged to the B&B owner, although he'd told her he didn't need anyone seeing to his comfort. Didn't need anyone to make his breakfast, empty his trash, change towels and sheets, or anything else. He simply wanted to rent the entire house and be left alone. Maybe she felt she had to be there to check him in and show him around, but he planned to send her packing as soon as that was done.

He filled Hitchcock's bowl with water. The dog lapped it up, splashing nearly half onto the floor. Alex got himself a bottle of the landlord's water from the refrigerator. It was cold, his wasn't, and he guessed it was there for guests. He drank half the water, left the rest on the kitchen island, and called Hitchcock to go with him upstairs.

He checked out the first two bedrooms at the top of the stairs, and down the hall he found a bathroom, and then…

He froze. A door appeared to be opening by itself.

I must be more tired from that drive than I thought.

It was the wind, he told himself. Old houses were breezy, and their doors often became lopsided over time.

As soon as he entered the room, he was drawn to the window with a magnificent view of the river. The cabin had been built on high land, and before him, bright green trees and shrubs interlaced with a blue ribbon of water. The view seemed to stretch for miles. He opened the window wide to let in a light breeze that carried a hint of pine. Sleeping here would be much better than he ever imagined.

He turned around and noticed a suitcase leaning against a chair, a pale blue sweatshirt tossed over the top. Just what part of having the entire place to himself didn't the owner understand? That was unfair. Probably the owner had stayed here readying the place for him. He'd left his own suitcase by the bedroom door.

He looked in the closet and bureau drawers—all empty—so it wasn't as if he'd barged into a room already occupied by someone else. And since he had rented the whole house, he moved the owner's suitcase and sweatshirt into the hall.

Hitchcock jumped onto the queen-size bed and sprawled across the foot, taking up nearly a third of the space.

The dog had the right idea. Alex joined his pal, fluffing a frilly pillow under his head and taking in his surroundings. The room had old-fashioned wallpaper in a soft yellow and white striped pattern, delicately carved furniture painted the color of cream, and a floral yellow and green bedspread. It was all too feminine for his taste, but he had to admit the room felt warm and welcoming.

He smirked at the thought of what some of the guys from his old Army unit would say if they could see him in a place like this. But then his grin vanished.

That was long ago. Another time.

A time before he began a series of missteps that caused his life to fall apart. If he was lucky, being here might be a start to making things right again. If that were even possible.

Hitchcock had been watching every one of Alex's moves, but now his eyes were closed and Alex heard his deep, throaty snoring. He was comfortable in these surroundings.

Alex's own back and legs ached after having spent so many hours driving, and now he nudged Hitchcock over to make room for his six-foot-three-inch frame.

He found the bed surprisingly comfortable, but unlike Hitchcock, he couldn't sleep.

His mind raced. He was glad not to be in Boston today. It was the wedding day of his ex-wife, Francine. His feelings for her had died sometime ago, but he still felt a profound sadness when he thought of how their marriage had begun with so much love and hope, and how, step-by-step, it had dissolved into bitterness.

He should have known better than to trust a lawyer, even if

he was married to her. The irony of that thought should have made him smile. But it hurt too much.

All he knew was that he had hoped for so much more out of their marriage. And worse, a lot more out of himself. Perhaps *he* was his biggest disappointment.

As usual.

And with that thought, his eyes shut.

CHAPTER 2

Carly shoved the car door closed with her hip and, despite her arms being laden with groceries, managed to unlock the cabin's front door. Glad to be here, she could almost feel relief lifting the weight of the world from her shoulders as she entered.

She was halfway across the great room when she noticed an open bottle of water next to her laptop. She stopped.

How had it gotten there?

She knew the front door had been locked. The French doors were closed tight, and she saw no obvious signs of a break in. Earlier she had seen no evidence of anyone living here. So, how did…?

Obviously, she had left it there, although she couldn't remember drinking any water. But then, she was exhausted after the long drive from San Francisco.

No sooner had she thought that and continued toward the kitchen than she gasped. An old-fashioned Mr. Coffee maker now sat on the countertop next to the expensive single-cup unit, and an enormous sack of dog food was on the floor propped against a cabinet door. Also on the floor was a dog's water bowl—with water puddling on the surrounding floor.

What in the world...?

Nervously, she peered from side to side, as if afraid of what she might see, all the while keeping her ears alert for any strange sounds. The cabin was quiet. But someone obviously had been in here.

Putting the bags along with her purse and keys on the kitchen island, she checked to make sure the French doors were still locked. They were. This was crazy. She opened the refrigerator door to put away the food that needed to stay cold or frozen, and every muscle in her body went taut.

Apples, melon slices, prepackaged sandwiches, and bottled water in a brand she had never bought now cluttered shelves that had been empty when she left for the store.

Someone was here … or had been here.

But who?

Moving as fast as she could, she shoved her groceries inside, then quietly closed the door in case the intruder or intruders were still here … and somehow, hadn't yet heard her in the house. Whoever had been here must have left when they heard her return. Squatters, maybe.

What should she do? Phone the sheriff? Run out of here?

A strange thumping sounded upstairs.

It made the decision for her. *Run!*

But then a thought struck, and she heaved a sigh of relief. It must be her sister Julia. Sure. That would make sense.

She had tried several times to phone Julia to tell her she was going to the cabin, but Julia never answered or called her back despite the many messages she'd left. If Julia was in the mountains of Idaho—like staying here at their cabin—that would explain her silence.

But then she heard more movement, even footsteps, from upstairs. Julia wasn't that heavy-footed.

That did it! She grabbed her car keys and handbag from the island. Confrontation wasn't in her DNA.

She was rushing across the room when a dog—a monster of a dog—launched itself down the stairs to the front door. It stopped there and faced her, its big jaws slightly open and its pink tongue hanging out as it panted.

She stopped on a dime. That so-called dog was bigger than she was! "Nice doggy! Nice, nice doggy," she said as she cautiously backed up.

Fortunately, the dog's huge fluffy tail wagged.

Then it sat, blocking the entire doorway.

"Go away," she said, hoping it would move so she could escape. "Go away. Shoo!"

A deep, rumbling "woof" was its reply. And now it was drooling. Carly didn't know if the beast normally did that, or if it was seeing her as a tasty treat.

"Who's down there?" a male voice shouted from upstairs.

Carly jumped backward, filled with thoughts of running into the backyard and hopping the fence. Unfortunately, her feet didn't share her thoughts and stayed rooted to the spot.

A man bounded down the stairs. Although his shoulders were broad, he was fairly slim. His dark brown hair was wavy, and his large eyes were a brilliant green. He was, frankly, good looking. "Oh, sorry! You must be … uh …"

"The cabin's owner?" she suggested, her voice filled with nervousness and sarcasm.

"Of course. I realized that." He rubbed his forehead. "Again, my apologies. I'm obviously still half asleep." The puffiness about his eyes and the way he was blinking from the light made him look as if he'd just woken up. "It was a long drive." He tried to smile, to sound friendly. "Somewhere around Nebraska I thought I'd die of old age before that long, flat road ever ended. Once here, I fell asleep until I heard my dog growling. I didn't mean to scare you."

Scared? Maybe she had looked scared, but no more. This stranger with his dour expression and weird diatribe about sleeping and driving made no sense to her. She glowered at him, hands on hips. "All that doesn't explain who you are or why you're *in my cabin!*"

His brows furrowed. "But you're the one who told me to just come in when I got here."

"No!"

He studied her as if he thought she might be addled. "I'm Alex Townson."

"I'm sorry, but—"

"Today is the first day of my rental."

Her stomach did a free fall. "Oh, my." His presence began to make sense. "You did say … rental?"

He scowled. "Look, I've already paid you a cleaning deposit and a substantial pet fee. If you're pulling some kind of scam here, I don't like it. I've got the signed agreement in my suitcase."

She couldn't believe what she was hearing. "You've rented the cabin?" she asked, hoping he might give her a different answer this time.

He gawked for a moment. "The YourB&B rental? You remember, don't you? I mean, you are …?"

"Julia?" Carly suggested.

"Julia, of course." Alex nodded. "We emailed several times, you may recall."

"No. I mean, no, I'm not Julia Perrin. She's my sister. My name is Carly Fullerton."

"But …" He looked confused and worried. "I have a signed contract for this cabin. I've come all the way, driving all the way, from Boston."

Carly's heart sank. She walked over to the sofa and sat down hard, hands clasped on her lap. Now what? She had expected to stay here for two weeks, rent free. She needed to stay here for two weeks, in fact.

Either that, or be homeless.

She took a deep breath. Years ago, her father had started a business, Carly's Catering. He'd named it after her, his "pride and joy," as he'd called her. When he passed away after a devastating illness, Carly was only age twenty-two, but she had quit college and took over the business, having inherited it along with her father's many medical bills. The business was never a big money maker, but lately her San Francisco rents had tripled and, despite her working longer and longer hours, she was falling further behind. Her stress level was through the roof, and along with fatigue, her doctor told her she needed complete rest or she would do serious damage to her health.

Another caterer, Dom Delucci, heard of her predicament. He wanted to test his ability to expand his business and offered to work her few contracted events over the next two weeks if he could rent her commercial kitchen at a big discount for that period. She had gladly accepted his offer. But, since her living quarters were in the back room of that kitchen, if she couldn't live in the cabin, she had nowhere else to go.

She told herself not to panic. Most people did weekend rentals. If nothing else, she could live in her car for two nights.

But she noticed his eyes narrow. He spoke slowly. "Am I correct in guessing your sister didn't tell you I'd rented this place for a month?"

"A month?" she gasped. *No! No way!*

His lips tightened. "I'm supposed to have the entire house all to myself. I need quiet."

"But an entire month?"

"With no disruptions."

This was insane. She stood, wringing her hands, doing all she could to gather strength. Looking at him scowling at her, she would need it. How had she ever thought him good-looking?

She sucked in her breath and then, calmly, as if she were the voice of reason, said, "Well, I'll only need the cabin for two weeks, you see, and once I leave, you can have the whole place to yourself. I'm sure we can find you other accommodations for that time, and I'll have my sister reimburse you, of course."

He folded his arms. "I'm sorry, but no."

She flung her hands toward him. It looked like she was pleading, which she didn't like, except that she was. "Why not? It's a rental. One place is as good as another."

"That's not my experience." His mouth tightened.

She dropped her arms. Why was he being so obstinate?

"I had difficulty finding a place that fit my needs," he said as he crossed to the French doors and looked out at the backyard and mountains beyond. "I wanted a place as different from Boston as I could find, and secluded. So no one will even know I'm here."

Her breath caught as she thought of all the murder mysteries she had read, her favorite and basically only form of entertainment. What was he not telling her? There was something about the way he carried himself, shoulders stiff, back straight, his eyes never quite still, that gave him the look of a man who knew danger. She gulped. "Are you … in hiding?"

He looked at her as if she might have two heads. "Of course not! I need peace and quiet so I can write my book."

That made some sense, she guessed. "What kind of book?"

"What does it matter?" He was close to shouting, his arms spread. "I paid for this rental. I have a contract. I believed your sister and drove here, expecting accommodations! If you have a problem, it seems you need to take it up with her, not with me."

"You don't have to yell." Her tone was arch. "I'm right here."

"And you seem incapable of going away!" He paced.

He was truly getting on her nerves. "I'm sorry about this

rental mix-up, I am. But circumstances are such that I have nowhere else to go. Plus, this is my property as much as Julia's, and I had no idea she was renting it out. You'll need to leave. I will, of course, help you find another place."

Alex stopped his panther-like pacing. One eyebrow arched. "Oh?"

Her chin jutted out. "That's what I said."

"Okay, fine. Let's see what kind of luck you have finding a place for me and Hitchcock." He pointed to his dog. "A purebred Newfoundland, all one-hundred-sixty pounds of him."

He acted as if the dog would be a challenge. She glanced at the big fellow, now lying down in front of the front door and drooling—a puddle of slobber drenched the hardwood under his chin—and realized the man might be right. Finding a place for her unwanted guest and his beastly companion might not be as easy as she hoped. "Shouldn't be *too* hard to find a place, Mr...." Suddenly her mind was a sieve. "I'm sorry, what did you say your name was? I'll need to know it when I find another room for you."

"Alex. Townson." His tone was beyond short. "I suggest you save yourself trouble and accept that I'm not leaving. Hitch likes it here. I like it here. Or I did until about ten minutes ago."

She gritted her teeth. "I'm sure there's a clause in the contract that discusses cancellation for unforeseen circumstances or acts of God."

He gazed heavenward. "You showing up here has nothing Godly about it. Quite the opposite, from my point of view. Please, Ms. Fullerton, look at the contract. Seems to me, if anyone's leaving, it's you."

"But I can't."

"Can't or won't? In any case, it's your problem, not mine." With that, he turned on his heel and went upstairs.

Carly was flabbergasted. If he were a decent fellow, he'd realize that since she was an owner and had every right to be here, he needed to respectfully gather his belongings and go away. Far away. Maybe upstairs, he'd realize that.

But instead he came back downstairs swinging Hitchcock's leash. He clipped it to the dog's collar and headed for the door. "We're going for a hike," he said, his tone cold. "When I get back, I'll expect to have the cabin all to myself, just as your sister and I agreed."

Think! Think! Carly had to get rid of her loathsome renter, but she didn't know what was in the rental contract. She needed to talk to Julia, which was easier said than done. So far, Julia had ignored all messages to call her back.

Since Carly's cell phone now showed no service, she used the cabin's landline. This time Julia picked up.

"Ah ha! So you can answer your phone," Carly said.

"Carly? Why are you calling me from the cabin?" Julia demanded.

Carly realized Julia's caller ID must have shown the cabin's number. "I planned to spend a couple of weeks here. Instead, I find you've rented the place out. How could you do that? Why didn't you tell me?"

"Since when do you care anything about the cabin?" Julia's tone was petulant, which was nothing new. Julia could sound crabby when she announced that the day was warm and sunny. "You've never cared about it before, and I'm not psychic. I'm surprised you could even find the place. You sure didn't want to help me fix it up."

"Maybe because I have a business to run." Carly sounded every bit as irritated as Julia.

"Oh, excuse me," Julia intoned. "You're a business owner, while I'm just a working stiff. Is that it?"

Carly rolled her eyes. They weren't off to a pleasant start. As usual. "Julia, I didn't call to argue."

"But you do it so well."

Carly silently counted to five. "Let's forget it and concentrate on my problem. Like, what am I supposed to do with this renter? He plans to be here a whole month."

"Frankly, I can't believe *you're* there." Julia sounded calmer. "I don't remember the last time you left your catering business for over twenty-four hours."

"My business is the reason I'm here," Carly confessed. "I've been working too much, too hard. 'Burn-out' my doctor calls it. I need to rest. And to figure out what to do with the business."

"What do you mean?" Julia sounded concerned. "Carly's Catering is your livelihood."

"Right now, it's not much of one. I need to either sell it or come up with a way to grow it."

"I'm sorry to hear that."

Had Julia just used the word "sorry"? Carly couldn't remember her sister ever sympathizing with her. But instead of voicing any appreciation of the sentiment, she brushed off the comment in her typical "I-can-handle-everything-alone" fashion. "I'll figure something out. But now, I've got a tenant problem. And he's got a dog."

"My being okay with the dog was a big reason he rented the place," Julia admitted. "I simply added an extra fee to the standard YourB&B contract. All I ask is you don't throw him out. YourB&B doesn't take well to customer complaints. This is only our second rental with them, and the first was a no-show. If he complains, that would be a major black mark against the cabin. I'd love to make enough money from vacation rentals to at least pay the property taxes, and maybe even show a little profit."

Carly frowned. "I guess I never thought much about the cost involved in keeping the place."

"No, you haven't."

"Anyway, the renter has got to go."

"No. You do."

"I sublet my place. I've got no home to return to."

"Well, you live in San Francisco where they apparently make life quite comfortable for homeless people, so—"

"Jules!"

"You know I'm kidding! But maybe the old ghosts will act up and they'll scare him away."

"If that happened, they'd scare me away, too!" Carly insisted. "So forget it."

"I wish you'd have told me your plans when you left messages on my phone. I thought you were calling to harass me about how much money I'd spent to fix up the cabin and clear the land around it. I thought I did pretty well, considering how little money we'd inherited."

"I take it there's nothing left?"

"I even broke into my own piggy bank. That's another reason I didn't want to listen to any complaints about it."

"I'm sorry, Jules," she said.

"Yeah. We're a sorry bunch, aren't we?"

Sadly, that was all too true. Whenever the three sisters had to deal with each other, which they all tried to avoid doing, "issues" tended to surface.

They surfaced over the phone as well, but Julia gave her the names and numbers of some rental agencies since Carly had no Internet access at the cabin, and soon, they said their goodbyes.

She sat at the bottom of the stairs with the big black phone on her lap and began contacting the agencies. She found several vacancies, and all but one refused to take a Newfoundland, no matter how well-trained she claimed he was. The one exception strangely lost phone service as they spoke. The call was not only disconnected, but when she called back a message announced that the line was no longer in service. It made no sense. She tried a few more times, but eventually gave up.

Renting a place for herself, she quickly discovered, was out of the question. Vacation rentals cost far more than renting an apartment. There was no way she could afford one. Her budget was already stretched to almost nothing to take these two weeks off.

With her lodger and his dog still out for a walk, she made a cup of coffee and sat on the sofa trying to come up with options. But almost immediately she heard the front door open, and then Hitchcock stood in front of her, panting, drooling, and looking up at her with soulful brown eyes. Her heart melted, and she patted his broad head.

"Well?" Alex also suddenly stood before her, but instead of heart-melting, his green eyes were cold, hard and questioning. "Did you find a place to stay?"

"Me?" She scoffed and rose to her feet. His question was so infuriating she was glad she was tall enough that she didn't have to tilt her head too far back to look him in the eyes. "You mean, did I find a place for you and *your horse* to stay?"

His mouth scrunched, and he nodded. "You could say that."

She sighed and sat back down. "It seems no one wants an elephant-size dog on their property."

Alex sat beside her, and just as quickly, the spacious sofa seemed much smaller. "I could have told you that." His look was filled with understanding. Not quite pity, but close. "I guess I should have warned you that the appeal of this cabin wasn't the only reason Hitchcock and I came all the way to a place in Idaho no one's ever heard of."

"And that's supposed to make me feel better?" she asked hotly.

To her surprise, his lips upturned and a slight crinkle of a smile softened his face. It made him seem less annoying. "I guess not. And your temper is living up to what they say about redheads."

She gaped at him as her hands automatically went to her hair. It was pulled back in a ponytail, and she tucked a few loose strands behind her ears.

He then sauntered into the kitchen and opened the refrigerator door. "I suppose most of the food in here isn't for a famished guest from Massachusetts."

She hurried after him. "That's right. It's mine." She didn't mean to sound peevish, but he clearly brought out the worst in her.

He shut the refrigerator door, remaining in front of it. "That's what I was afraid of." He sounded almost sad.

And she realized she was hungry. She had planned an easy meal—a simple fettuccine Alfredo, a green salad, and French bread. She rummaged around the cabinets until she found a pasta-size pot, filled it with water, and put it on the stove.

She then walked to the refrigerator and glared at him. He not only got out of her way, but even opened the door for her. With a curt, "Thanks," she took out butter, parsley, cream, Parmesan cheese, and lettuce for a salad.

"You know how to cook or something?" he asked. She couldn't help but notice the way he hungrily ogled the food— and realized with more than a little distress that no man had ever looked at her with such longing.

"Or something," she grumbled.

"That food sure looks good." Alex moved closer. He looked like he might start drooling as badly as Hitchcock did.

"It's from *the local grocery store*." She side-stepped away from him. *Hint, fella!*

"You know," he said as his gaze jumped from her to the package of fettuccine noodles she was opening, "according to the terms of my rental agreement, I could demand you leave here immediately. But I'm actually a nice fellow, and way too tired after that long trip from Boston to work on my novel this evening, so it doesn't matter that you're here disturbing me. I'll let you stay tonight. Tomorrow, however, I want you out."

She washed some parsley, then picked up a knife and began to mince it. Vigorously. "It is my cabin, remember?"

"But it's my rental contract."

"Possession is nine-tenths of the law."

He shrugged. "Tell it to the judge, lady."

"*Hah!*"

With a woeful sigh, he opened the refrigerator door and studied its contents. Finally, he took out a cellophane-wrapped ham-and-cheese sandwich. Even through the wrapping, the bread looked drier than the Sahara. She guessed he'd bought it at a gas station food mart. The sandwich looked so pathetic that, irritating as he was, she couldn't help but feel sorry for him. And, if she were being honest about it, this situation really wasn't his fault.

"Put that back," she said. "I can easily make enough dinner for two."

"And I"—he raised his eyebrows—"don't need anyone taking care of me. This is just fine."

"Suit yourself." She gave a one-shoulder shrug. "But you're going to miss out on a fine dinner."

"And a scintillating conversation, I'm sure."

She arched an eyebrow. "Only if I talk to myself."

"Ouch!" He seemed unable to stop a small smile as he took his sandwich and a bottle of water and went out to the back porch to eat his "dinner."

Seriously? That man was even more pigheaded than she thought.

Carly sprinkled lots of extra Parmesan cheese onto her pasta, then put her dinner plate, utensils, and iced tea onto a tray and carried it upstairs. She'd rather eat in her bedroom than be anywhere near Alex-blankety-blank-Townson.

At the top of the stairs, the first thing she saw was her suitcase standing upright in the middle of the hallway and her sweatshirt neatly folded on top of it. Black and red spots of sheer fury danced before her eyes.

What nerve!

She put her tray on the floor and stormed into the river-view room.

The bedspread had been tossed aside, and the covers pulled back, making it look as if *that man* had lain on her clean sheets. She was beyond furious.

His suitcase stood in a corner. She picked it up. It felt light—too light. He didn't, did he?

Opening a bureau drawer, *her* bureau drawer, she saw his underwear in it, neatly folded. In the closet, jackets, shirts, and trousers hung, all sorted by color, no less.

She folded her arms. She'd like to hang him! And what kind of psycho was he? Who in the world folded their BVDs?

Wheeling her suitcase, she marched into the bedroom at the far end of the hall, as far away from him as possible.

She would sleep there that night, but tomorrow she'd get rid of that … that bedroom-stealing interloper!

No sooner had she finished her dinner than she heard the garage door open, the revving of an automobile, and soon after, the door closing. He left the cabin. Could it be for good? Had he relented?

Filled with hope, she crept back downstairs. But when she entered the great room, Hitchcock was sleeping on the sofa and nothing else had changed. No way would Alex Townson have gone off and abandoned his dog. He'd be back.

With a heavy sigh, she spun around to stare at Elijah

Donnelly's portrait, unable to shake the feeling he was laughing at her. How she hated those creepy purple eyes of his.

But she now saw a normal, old-fashioned portrait. She pressed her palms to her forehead. Her doctor had warned her that her nerves were so frayed she might start over-reacting to situations, even—potentially—imagining things. A laughing ghost in a portrait? What next? Would he fly around the room with a sheet over him? She had to get a grip.

She quickly cleaned up the kitchen, made herself some coffee, and went back upstairs.

She changed into comfortable flannel pj's, perfect for chilly mountain nighttime air, and climbed into bed. She wasn't about to unpack her suitcase. Somehow, she would get that river-view room if it was the last thing she did. Soon, she shut off the light.

But Alex Townson still hadn't returned, and she couldn't help but wonder if he had gone to a bar in town. This was, she suddenly realized, Saturday night. When she was a girl, the town of Crouch always had country-western music and dancing all weekend long. She imagined it still did, with lots of young, single people having fun. But here she was—young, single, and in bed alone before ten o'clock.

What a loser!

She turned onto her side, pounded the pillow a few times to make it more comfortable, and shut her eyes. She tried not to listen for noises, like the sound of the renter returning to the cabin. What a shame, she told herself, for such a good-looking man with such broad shoulders and lose-yourself-in-them gorgeous green eyes, to be such an irritating jerk. With that thought, she fell asleep.

CHAPTER 4

Earlier that same evening when Alex went out onto the deck with his gas station food mart sandwich, he had tried to ignore the sounds of Carly cooking in the kitchen and the mouth-watering scent of creamy, garlic-laced fettuccine Alfredo and French bread warmed in the oven. He took a couple bites of his sandwich, but it was hard to eat while drooling over something else. He threw away a greenish spot on the bread and gave the rest of the sandwich to Hitchcock.

He watched Carly go upstairs carrying a tray with her dinner.

Who needs dinner? A little fasting is good for the soul, they say. Whoever 'they' are. He lounged back on a chair. But as he sat, he grew more and more hungry.

Finally, he got his car out of the garage and drove into Crouch. He went up and down the main drag and there wasn't a fast food place to be found. What kind of town was this? There were a couple of places that looked like they served food, but he had no idea what time anything closed.

A place called the Rusty Nail, a brew pub, appealed to him.

Drinks and food were exactly what he needed. Especially the drinks part.

He went inside to find an old-fashioned looking Western bar and restaurant. He took a stool at the bar while he checked the place out. A white-haired bartender with an equally white mustache strolled over. "What can I get you?" he drawled.

"Whiskey on the rocks." Alex didn't need anything pretentious, just something strong enough to calm his overwrought nerves.

"You visiting our little town a while?" the bartender asked as he poured the drink.

"I am. A whole month, in fact."

"Good. You'll enjoy it, I think. The name's Butch, by the way."

"Alex."

"So, you hunt?"

"No."

"Fish?"

"No. I just want a little quiet." Alex felt the need to explain. "Something different from Boston, where I live."

"You've come to the right place for quiet, that's for sure," Butch said with a firm nod. "Where you staying?"

"I lucked out. Great location by the river, at the end of a long dirt road."

"Hmm. A bed and breakfast, is it? North of town?"

"I guess it's north. I guess it could be a bed and breakfast, but I rented the whole house. I rarely eat breakfast anyway."

"Funny. I don't recall any places to stay off a dirt road there." Then a strange expression came over his face. "Unless ..." His lips clamped shut, and he picked up a dishrag and started wiping down the bar.

"Unless?" Alex asked, curious now.

"Well, there's one place I know was just fixed up recently.

The old Donnelly cabin. But I don't think they'd be renting it out."

"No? Why not?"

Butch looked from side to side as if to make sure no one was listening, then leaned close and in a hushed voice said, "They say the place is haunted. How'd that be for giving the cabin—and the town—a bad reputation?"

Alex snorted. "The only one haunting the cabin I'm in is the foul-tempered owner. No ghost would stand a chance around her."

Butch chuckled.

Alex decided he'd had enough town gossip. He'd been watching a parade of huge burgers and fries go by as he sat at the bar. They were nothing fancy, but looked and smelled so delicious, he could hear his stomach growling. He finished his drink. "I think I'll move over to a table and have some dinner. If you'd send another whiskey and a menu my way, that'd be great."

It didn't take long before the burger he ordered was delivered. It was as tasty as it smelled, and the whiskey went down smoothly.

Alex tried to relax, tried not to dwell on what had driven him away from Boston, but to concentrate on the book he needed to write.

But his wayward thoughts instead zeroed in on the puzzle that was Carly Fullerton. She obviously was low on funds, or she would have turned around and left when she realized that he had rented the cabin. He kept telling himself nothing about this situation was his fault, and that she wasn't his problem. But she had looked so crestfallen to learn she'd have to leave, he actually felt sorry for the kid.

He had to stop this. Feeling sorry for people was what had caused all his problems. In fact, if he could have cut that part out of his heart, out of his soul, he'd still be married. He shook his head. What did that say about his choice in women?

CHAPTER 5

Carly breathed a sigh of relief the next morning when she stepped into the great room and saw that it was empty. That meant she didn't have to immediately face Alex as she made herself a cup of coffee. It should help her feel more human, and then she could try to come up with a solution to this awkward rental situation. Or so she hoped.

She had dressed more professionally than the day before. White slacks instead of jeans and a nicely fitting teal top instead of a baggy T-shirt might make her words carry more authority. She even put on makeup and had pulled her red hair sleekly back into a sophisticated knot. Since he had foolishly made reference to redheads having bad tempers, she'd show him just how much of a temper she had!

If Mr. I-Want-To-Be-Alone wanted a fight, she was ready to give him one.

She had just sat down at the kitchen island with her coffee when the cabin's telephone rang. She ran to pick it up, hoping it hadn't awakened her renter.

"Hello."

"Hi. It's Mallory."

Carly was shocked. Her youngest half-sister never called her. "What a surprise to hear from you."

"Julia called last night. She told me what happened, and said she wanted to make sure I wasn't planning a surprise trip to the cabin, too!" There was way too much mischief in Mallory's voice. Typical Mallory. "I tell you, she didn't sound the least bit amused."

Great, Carly thought. Now even her younger sister was poking fun at her. Somehow she managed to speak with a clenched jaw. "This situation isn't the least bit funny. Or are you calling to offer me your Manhattan apartment?"

"Hah! No way. But are things as desperate as Julia said? She made it sound as if you might need to close up your business. I was sorry to hear it."

Carly wasn't used to hearing any level of concern about her life or feelings from anyone and hadn't since her father died. First Julia had sounded concerned, and now Mallory's simple words touched her heart. Still, she couldn't admit the problem. With a stiff upper lip, she said, "It's not that bad. I'll find a way to keep it going."

"That's the spirit!" Mallory said. "In fact, this morning I came up with an idea about the cabin's rental. I called to run it past you."

"I'm open for anything at this point," Carly said, and as she thought about Alex Townson, added, "Legal or not."

Mallory chuckled lightly. "Ideally, the ghosts will see that he leaves."

"So far, they've been quiet, or nonexistent, which is the most likely case."

"Or, they like him," Mallory suggested.

"Or maybe I need to help him join them!"

With a chuckle, Mallory said, "Let's hope you don't have to go that far. But the point is, he rented the house off of a listing on YourB&B, which means it's a bed and breakfast."

"Maybe technically, but he booked it as a rental, not a B&B," Carly explained.

"I looked at the cabin's listing and although it says it's a vacation rental, it doesn't specifically say the owner doesn't live on the premises and doesn't serve breakfast—and both come with the territory when one rents a bed and breakfast."

"But he and Julia apparently agreed it was a simple rental of the whole house."

"Perhaps, but Julia used the standard YourB&B contract and didn't change it." Mallory stressed the point, adding, "I work in real estate in New York City, which is as tough as it gets when dealing with people. And everyone knows when there's an issue, what's in writing counts. So I suggest you tell the renter you'll be serving him breakfast each day and, like most B&B owners, you'll be living on the premises. He can take it or leave it."

Carly's jaw dropped at the suggestion, and it took her a moment before she could even reply. The idea was insane. Outrageous. Glorious. "Mallory, you're a genius!"

"Yeah, I know. Be sure to tell me how it turns out."

"Definitely." It was time to be nice, Carly told herself, wracking her brain for the last information Mallory had given her. "And how's Dennis?"

"Long gone. But Rodney is fine."

Rodney? Had she heard about Rodney? "Well great! Are you serious about him?"

"Not really."

That was a surprise. Mallory was usually engaged to *someone*, but she had never yet walked down the aisle. Carly decided not to pursue the matter, but simply said, "Gotta run. Thank you so much for the advice!"

She no sooner ended the call than she heard some movement from upstairs and decided there was no time like the present to put Mallory's plan into place. A hearty breakfast ought to do the trick, and thankfully she'd already bought all the ingredients she needed.

Soon, she heard the unmistakable sound of Hitchcock racing down the stairs, followed by Alex's footsteps. She heard him talking to Hitchcock. "Okay, no chasing birds or squirrels or grizzly bears. Just a quick walk, then you'll get breakfast."

With a sigh of relief when the front door closed, she put on a bibbed apron and went to work on the pancake batter and pork sausage.

"Fried or scrambled," she called out when she heard the two return.

"You aren't talking about eggs, are you?" Alex asked, walking across the great room, a slight frown on his face.

"What else?" she said flatly, although she had wanted to sound friendly, or at least amiable.

"I'm a toast and coffee kind of guy in the morning."

She aimed a forced smile at him. "Great. Fried it is. Over easy, which is the best way to serve them with pancakes."

"Wait, *pancakes?*"

She tried not to look at him as she expertly did a one-handed crack of two eggs into a pan sizzling with butter. Still, she couldn't help but notice that the brisk morning air had brought a healthy color to his cheeks and left his dark hair alluringly tousled. She swallowed hard, wishing she hadn't noticed how his green pullover brought out the color of his eyes, or how the slight darkening along his cheeks, as if he were growing a beard, was quite a good look on him. Too bad he was so completely annoying.

Hitchcock sprawled on the floor right behind her. In her way, of course, but who could find fault with a dog who looked up at her with such soulful eyes?

"What is all this?" Alex asked, sitting on one of the bar stools. "And who said you could use my kitchen again?"

"They say food's good for the soul." She was trying to stay civil. "And I hate cooking just for one."

He eyed the food as she cooked, and she wondered if he had any idea how much his face revealed that he liked what he was seeing. "You're willing to feed someone who's throwing you out of the cabin?"

"*My* cabin." She gave him a stiff smile. Reminding herself of the old saw that the way to a man's heart is through his stomach, she filled a large, cobalt blue pottery mug with coffee and slid it in front of him. "Cream? Sugar?"

"Black."

As his heart, she thought. "You may be a toast-only kind-of-guy, but once you've tasted my lemon and blueberry pancakes, you'll drool for more."

"I've always preferred buckwheat."

"You're being contrary."

"How else should a guy be who's kicking you out of your own home?"

She ignored his comment. Before long she set an overflowing plate before him, drizzled some genuine maple syrup over the pancakes, and refilled his cup with coffee. "You don't mind if I join you, do you?"

He looked up at her through impossibly long lashes. "I guess that's one way of making sure you didn't poison this."

"Oh, that's funny. You're a regular Don Rickles." Once her cooking had started melting his cold, cold heart, if that were even possible, she'd hit him with Mallory's plan.

"Guess I'll take my chances." He dug his fork into the pancakes and lifted a hefty serving toward his mouth. He stared at the fluffy concoction dripping with syrup for a long moment, flashed her a questioning glance, then shoveled the forkful into his mouth. He chewed thoughtfully and then, a hesitant smile on his face, admitted, "It is pretty good."

"Better than pretty good. Amazing."

"Sure of yourself, aren't you?"

She wished. "Only where cooking is concerned—and gardening. What about you? What are you amazing at?"

"Writing. When I'm alone. When I have total quiet and no interruptions."

So much for friendly banter.

They ate in silence after that. It was all she could do to swallow each mouthful. He seemed to stare off in space, and she did the same. It was just about the most uncomfortable few minutes she'd ever spent sitting across from a good-looking man.

Not until he sopped up every speck of food on his plate with the last remaining piece of pancake, did she decide the time had come to speak up. She took a healthy swallow of coffee to steel her nerves then, elbows on the counter, she looked him dead in the eye. "I've been thinking about the situation we find ourselves in."

"We?" he asked. "Or you?"

She steeled herself. "I have a proposal to make." Her words were soft, measured.

He wiped his mouth with a napkin then placed it on his plate, his gaze unreadable.

She sucked in a deep breath. "At most bed-and-breakfast establishments, the owner lives on the property, serves a big breakfast, and once breakfast is over, the guests have the run of the public parts of the house while the owner stays out of the way."

He frowned and reached for his coffee.

She cleared her throat. "The cabin is, in fact, a bed-and-breakfast, and I'd like to operate it as such. Although you'll be giving up a little privacy, I'll put on the coffee first thing, and when you'd like to eat, I'll prepare a big breakfast for you. Scones, muffins, omelets, and so on. I'll even stock the refrigerator with homemade treats and snacks, selecting those foods you most enjoy. And, of course, you'll be free to use the kitchen to make yourself dinner or whatever you wish throughout the day."

Surprise filled his face, but soon his eyes narrowed. That reaction didn't look good. Something told her she'd blown it.

"You'll scarcely know I'm here," she added quickly. "There are three upstairs bedrooms. You can have the river view room and the extra one for an office, or whatever. I'll take the one I'm in now. It's the smallest."

He continued to frown.

"You'll have the entire downstairs. We must share the upstairs bathroom, since it's the only one with a shower. I'll have to use the kitchen, of course. And it'll only be for two weeks while I'm here. I'll try my best to stay invisible, completely out of sight. After that, the entire place will be yours."

He leaned back in his chair. "So that's the reason for this IHOP impersonation."

She felt her face turn fiery under his green-eyed stare. "It wasn't an impersonation. I've just proven to you that I can make a quality meal. And rest assured, I'll give you the same quality every morning you're a guest here."

He smirked. "Oh, I'm a 'guest' now, am I?"

"Of course!" Nose high, she added, "A welcome guest."

Even though it seemed impossible, his frown deepened. "I just don't know."

She drew in a deep breath, reminding herself that she was a businesswoman, and this was a business transaction—sexy green eyes or not. And he seemed to be weakening. "I'll even help with Hitchcock when you're too busy to walk him."

For a moment, looking at his expression, she hoped he was relenting. But then he said, "If it were just me, I'd say we try it. But it isn't. There are people depending on me to get this book finished soon. But so far, nothing is working. I really hoped that here things would be different. But I'll be working around the clock. No schedule, nothing. Just eat, sleep, and write. So, I'm sorry. I can't take the chance of being disturbed."

"And so am I." It was time to act tough. She hated acting tough. If she were her sister Julia, she'd have no problem throwing Alex Townson out of here. But she wasn't. Still, she forced herself to her feet, palms flat on the granite island, and leaned toward him, so close she could almost feel the heat of his breath. "Look at your contract! It doesn't exclude treating this rental as a B&B. And it doesn't matter what you and Julia verbally agreed to. The contract you signed is what covers this situation."

His face fell. "I was trying to be reasonable. But now, I've got work to do." He walked to the sofa, sat, and opened up his laptop. "I'm staying."

Carly glared at him. "And so am I."

CHAPTER 6

Alex couldn't stop himself from watching the cabin's owner as she cleaned up the kitchen. He felt like a first-class cad at the way he was talking to her, but he didn't feel he had a choice.

He needed her out of there, to have the cabin to himself, to have no distractions. And—as he'd noticed that morning—Carly Fullerton could easily become a distraction.

He'd been stunned when he saw her. Yesterday, she had looked frazzled, her clothes were grubby, and her temper short.

The temper was still a thing to behold, but beyond that, her red hair shone like a jewel, and he couldn't stop staring at her large, gray eyes. They intrigued him.

She intrigued him.

He wondered if that was why he was being so hard on her. Truth be told, he didn't need those two extra bedrooms, and to start the day with a good meal wasn't a bad idea at all. In fact, it could be quite a time-saver. So why hadn't he agreed to her B&B suggestion?

On the other hand, she had disrupted his plans so completely, he should detest her. Instead, he found he didn't even mind having her sit across from him as he ate an amazingly delicious breakfast that morning. And he never ate breakfast.

Clearly, there was something wrong with him.

Just then, he noticed that Carly had finished with the kitchen. He watched her march across the great room and go upstairs without a single glance his way.

Whoa, that was one pissed-off woman.

Not his problem.

He really needed to think about his novel.

But then he noticed a scent in the air. Lemons and blueberries lingered, although he had watched her clean up after breakfast and put everything away. Unbidden, his thoughts turned again to Carly, to her high cheekbones and delicate structure of her face. Her figure was, in a word, voluptuous. But most of all, he found himself lost in the depths of those eyes—even when they flashed with anger, which they seemed to do quite often around him.

He shook his head with disgust, wondering where all that had come from. Obviously, he'd been away from interesting female companionship for far too long.

And he was wasting time. He needed to concentrate on what he was here for. His novel.

He opened the file that was supposed to contain chapter one of his newest book and stared at a blank screen.

It had been blank for a couple of months now. During most of his career as a writer, how or when he wrote his books and what they had to "say" hadn't mattered all that much. He could churn out one of his international spy/thriller novels with ease. They were even fun to write. But suddenly, he had a lot riding on this next book—not only for himself but also for some innocent kids who were more important to him than anything else in his life—and the words just wouldn't come. Worse, the few words that did come were such garbage he deleted them almost as soon as he wrote them down.

He'd never had writer's block before—and hadn't even believed it existed. Until now. He had no idea how to get past it and sighed with frustration, wondering if he would ever again be able to write a book.

Carly felt as if someone were driving a stake into her forehead.

It had to be caffeine deprivation. She had tried to drink enough coffee at breakfast to tide her over throughout the day, but it was now three in the afternoon, and she needed a cup. Not only for her headache, but to keep her awake. She never knew books about how to profitably run a small business could be so mind-numbingly dull.

She slowly crept down the stairs, hoping she wouldn't bother her surly "guest." Guest, hah! He was even more irritating that morning than he'd been the day before. And her sister Mallory's plan about the cabin being a B&B had been a good one.

Now, she saw that he had pushed the dining table against the window and had moved all the chairs away from it except the one he sat on. He had turned it into his personal desk! The man truly had more nerve than brains.

And now sat there with lots of little stacks of colorful index cards all around him. His back was to her and, despite herself, she couldn't help but notice how the ivory, cable-knit pullover stretched across broad, muscular shoulders. He had rolled up the sleeves to reveal tanned forearms.

He picked up a card, read it, hovered it over the stacks until he decided which to place it on, and then picked up another card. She watched him go through a similar rigmarole two more times. What was he up to?

She was tiptoeing toward the kitchen when he turned around.

"I thought I felt a presence," he said.

She jumped. "A presence? Oh! You mean me." She tried to laugh off her jumpiness. "I'm getting myself a cup of coffee." She put a coffee pod into the machine, pressed the lever, and then listened to the machine grind and whirr. "I'll be out of here in a moment."

"Permanently, I hope," he said archly and returned to his index cards.

She made a wrinkled-nose, scrunched-mouth face at the back of his head, stopping short of sticking out her tongue, tempting though it be. It would serve him right if all those stupid cards were used in a game of 52-pickup. Taking the coffee cup, she decided to drink it outdoors rather than up in the bedroom which was already feeling claustrophobic. Maybe that was why she was so sleepy.

Hitchcock trotted over to her, looking up as if he wanted to go outside every bit as much as she did.

"Your dog seems to want to follow me outside, if that's okay," she said.

"No problem," he mumbled, concentrating on a purple card in his hand.

Coffee cup in one hand, she opened the French doors with the other and Hitch shot out. He was so large, he bumped the door Carly held, causing her to let go of it as it opened wide, and then he bumped into the other door, causing it to fling open as well.

At the same moment, the front door blew open and swung all the way around to land with a loud crash against the wall.

Alex nearly jumped out of his skin. "What the—?" He spun toward the door, feet firmly planted, body in a slight crouch, looking ready to go on the attack.

Carly gaped at how quickly he went all commando on her. What was with the guy? It was just a door.

But having both front and back doors open must have created a wind-tunnel because a mini-cyclone suddenly whooshed through the cabin, and lifted Alex's index cards high into the air, and swirled them around like Dorothy's house in the Wizard of Oz.

Alex tried to grab the cards, but they somehow flew out of his reach. Desperate, he threw himself onto the cards still on the table. But the cards somehow squeezed past him and also swooped around the room.

Carly couldn't move for a moment as she watched the bizarre scene unfold, but then she put down her coffee cup and tried to catch any cards that blew her way. They darted out of her reach as if with a mind of their own.

"Shut the door!" Alex yelled as he somehow plucked a single card from the air. Others zipped about even faster, like crazed whirling dervishes. Alex finally gave up trying to keep any cards on the tabletop and bolted across the room to the front door.

Carly grabbed the French door handles, one then the other, but then she saw Hitchcock running toward her to come back inside. "Hurry!" she called.

Alex reached the front door, but had to pull hard to get it to close.

As soon as Hitchcock was in, Carly yanked the French doors shut.

At that, the whirlwind stopped.

Carly, eyes wide and mouth agape, stared dumbfounded at the doors, at the way they seemed to spring open on their own and then remained that way as if by some unseen force. She took in the chaos Alex's cards had become. The cards that had appeared to be carefully sorted were now on the floor, on chairs, and a few had flown all the way across the room to the fireplace. As she contemplated her wish about the practical joke card game of "52 pickup," a cold chill soared through her from the top of her head down to her toes. No, she told herself. Impossible.

Alex stood in the center of the great room, one hand raking his hair, looking at the mess all around him. "What in the world just happened?"

"I … I don't know," she murmured. "A powerful gust of wind, maybe?"

Hitchcock sidled over to a thick pile of cards and, with a grunt, lay down on top of them.

"I'm guessing those cards are for your story." Carly's voice was tiny.

Alex shook his head. "They are. Or were." He sounded anguished. "At times like this, I wonder why I bother."

His level of dismay stunned her. She got down on her knees and began resolutely picking up the cards. "What's the reason for the colors?"

"Plot. Characters." He held out his hand to help her back up. "You don't have to do that."

She shook her head. "This mess wouldn't have happened if I hadn't disturbed you. I'm so sorry. I didn't mean—"

"Please don't." His voice was soft, caring, as he knelt down beside her and also began picking up cards. "It's not your fault. Maybe I didn't pull the door shut tight enough after my walk with Hitch this morning. It was just one of those things."

She didn't think so. Her mind filled with memories of Roxanne telling her and her sisters about the ghosts that haunted the Donnelly cabin. They liked to wreak havoc, but Roxanne never understood why they did the strange things they did.

Alex was so unhappy about his cards, she almost felt guilty. But guilt assumed culpability, as if the ghosts had done her bidding.

Of course they hadn't, Carly thought. But if the cabin's

ghosts did exist, they could have easily created this mess. Them, and her nonsensical wish. The more she thought about it, the more her head spun. I can't seriously be considering that ghosts did this, she told herself.

Suddenly, she felt light-headed and sat up, blinking fast and taking long, deep breaths.

Alex glanced at her, then also sat up and faced her. He took hold of her arm, as if fearing she might keel over. "Are you all right?"

She tried to act "normal," whatever that was. But instead, she slowly became aware of his nearness, too aware, which was crazy at a time like this, and about a man she didn't like. She was clearly losing it. She rubbed her forehead. "I'm fine," she murmured, then pulled her arm free.

He helped her to slowly stand as she took a few more deep breaths.

"See? No problem," she announced. Then noticing Hitchcock curled up on a bunch of cards, she took hold of the dog's collar and gave him a tug to get him to stand. "Now you can pick up those cards, too," she said a little too brightly.

"Thanks," he murmured.

"I think it might be easier if Hitch and I got out of your way for a while."

Alex studied her, worry written on his face, although she had no idea if it had to do with her or his index cards as he murmured, "Excellent idea."

CHAPTER 7

Alex was swearing beneath his breath and resorting the index cards when his phone rang.

The caller ID showed Jack Bellar, his agent. Bellar was one of the last people Alex wanted to talk to right now. Jaw tight, he answered.

"Alex, how is … coming?" Despite the way the phone cut out, Bellar sounded irritatingly upbeat.

"I just got here yesterday, Jack. Don't expect a miracle." Alex knew his voice sounded the opposite of upbeat.

"Maybe not … miracle, but … expect … thing."

Alex was tempted to use the poor cell service as an excuse to hang up, but when he went out to the backyard, his phone went up to two bars.

He put the phone back to his ear to find that Jack was still talking. "Your editor is close to having a meltdown. She needs at least a complete synopsis so they can start planning the cover and release activities. This book will make your career. Don't blow it."

Alex shut his eyes a moment, then said, "I know, but it's not jelled yet."

"How many words do you have so far?"

"I'm not sure."

"Not sure? Look, you aren't trying to be Dostoevsky here. You've already published five best-selling thrillers, and your editor hopes to push this next book to the *New York Times* list. And, frankly, so does your agent!"

Alex couldn't stop an exasperated tone of both fatigue and irritation. "Don't worry. I'll get it done."

"This is really important. How about we have a face-to-face? We can kick around some ideas—"

"I'm not in Boston, Jack. I'm in Idaho. Remember?"

"There are planes to Idaho."

Alex felt his stomach tighten. "Look, I'll have something for you in a few days, okay? Until then, just relax."

"I'm counting on you, Alex. And so is your publisher."

"Right," Alex muttered. He ran his free hand through the waves of his dark brown hair and heaved a weary sigh. In his mind he couldn't help but think, *Jack, you don't know the half of it.*

When Carly returned to the cabin with Hitchcock, she opened the front door a crack. "Is it safe?"

"Come in."

She entered the room to find Alex standing over the dining room table, the cards rubber banded together in only three stacks, with the colors completely mixed up.

Hitch ran up to Alex and looked up with sad eyes, a wet nose, and even wetter jowls as he nudged Alex's hand in greeting.

"Hello, boy," Alex said, then bent and rubbed Hitch's head with both hands. "Good to see you. You're a good dog. I wasn't mad at you, Hitch. I was mad at myself. As usual. Come on, let's find you a treat."

Hitch's tail wagged as he galumphed by Alex's side to the pantry.

"Is there anything I can do? Sort them by color, maybe?" Carly asked, eying the cards.

"Not really. I had an annoying phone call from my agent, and that set me back further than the breeze did."

She pulled a bottle of beer from the refrigerator and held it up. "Might this help?"

He couldn't help a small, weary smile. "Definitely."

She popped off the top and handed it to him, then got one for herself as he walked toward the French doors to the back porch.

The porch was now sheltered in a cool, inviting shade. But as a good B&B hostess, she forced herself toward her warm, upstairs bedroom.

"If you'd like to enjoy your beer outside," Alex said from the doorway, "it's okay."

Carly hesitated. But something made her glance up at Elijah Donnelly's portrait. He had one eyebrow lifted in curiosity. She did a double-take, but on second glance, the eyebrow was back in place. She swallowed. "I would, actually."

The wide porch held a long bench covered with cushions, with rattan chairs and end tables on each side of it. Steps from the porch led down to the backyard, and red hybrid tea rose bushes grew along the porch railing. Beyond them was a gravel walkway, and then a fenced acre of land.

Roxanne had dubbed the land "the orchard" because she had planted two apple and two pear trees out there. They were fully grown now, tall and healthy, and bore fruit each fall.

Alex sat at one end of the bench and stared out at the fruit trees, his expression somber. Even though every rational part of her insisted she had nothing to do with what had happened to his index cards, looking at him now, she felt increasingly guilty. She took the chair near him and after a while, asked, "Did that mess with your index cards cause the problem with your agent?"

He shook his head, looking chagrined. "No, not at all. Although, come to think of it, they might be a symbol of my problem."

"Oh?"

"I need to write a draft of my next book. That's what he called about."

"But you just got here," Carly said.

Alex rubbed the condensation on the beer bottle with his thumb. His voice was bitter. "Let's say he had the impression I'm further along than I am."

Again, she had to wonder what was troubling him so much. "A misunderstanding? With you?" She gave him a side-long glance and a small grin. "I can't imagine."

He smirked and rolled his eyes. "I should have known better than to admit such a thing to you."

She liked that he was still able to joke. "Probably. But if not the index cards, what is the problem?"

"Do you read thrillers?" he asked.

"I'm more into mysteries," she said. "But tell me anyway."

He nodded. A long while passed before he began to speak. "The problem has to do with my main character. Rip Tarrington is a former CIA agent, strong, forceful, and a loner. He travels the world fighting bad guys and having dalliances with beautiful women. Lots of them. He's a love 'em and leave 'em kind of guy."

She watched a genuine smile touch Alex's lips as he talked about his creation, a very nice smile, in fact. But then his expression changed.

"For my next book, my editor wants Rip to get serious about a woman. I mean, what is she thinking? It'll wreck the entire series."

He took a long swallow of his beer and then looked so

forlorn, it was all Carly could do to keep a straight face. "Why in the world would having him fall in love wreck your series?"

He gave her an astonished gaze that said she understood nothing about real men. "Rip Tarrington is supposed to go off and save the world. Is he suddenly supposed to ask his wife's permission before he leaves? Or is danger supposed to stop because he needs to change his kid's diaper?"

At that, she couldn't hide her smile. "Is that really how you see a serious relationship?"

"It's true!" he exclaimed, suddenly testy.

Her eyebrows rose. "Spoken like a man who's been married."

He shrugged and didn't answer.

Whatever was going on in that area, she decided she'd better change the subject. "Would you like another beer?"

He looked at his bottle, surprised to find it empty. "I shouldn't. I need a clear head when I work. I'd better get back inside."

She nodded, surprised to find she was sorry that this interlude had ended so soon.

They walked back into the house.

"Will you still be able to use the index cards?" she asked, with a nod toward much larger stacks he now had.

He scowled. "Who knows? Now that they're all scrambled, the story might finally be interesting enough to write."

She hurried back upstairs before he got over his aggravation at the index cards and focused it back at her.

CHAPTER 8

Carly did her best not to disturb Alex the rest of the day and evening. She half expected him to knock on her door and demand, again, that she leave the cabin.

When evening came, she went down the stairs and straight out the front door without even glancing in the great room and drove to town.

Since the Rusty Nail had Wi-Fi, she went there for dinner. She waved hello to Butch behind the bar, then got a table by herself and ordered a chili burger and a margarita.

As soon as she was alone, she used her phone to go to a book site and look up Alex Townson. His five thrillers about Rip Tarrington had garnered many good reviews from readers, as well as a few snarky ones, which she was sure must have driven Alex half crazy. She downloaded book one in the series. Know thy enemy, she told herself.

Then she read his bio. Was it real? He had been in Military Intelligence in the Army. What? Alex? And then, after leaving military service, he became a lawyer. Incredible.

The Army part made some sense when she thought about his perfect posture, his meticulously arranged clothing, and even his ready-for-action stance when the great room doors had banged open. But the lawyer part surprised her. She wondered if he was still a practicing attorney, or if he'd given that up to write.

Actually, if he were still practicing, the first words out of his mouth when he discovered her in the cabin would have been, "I'll sue."

Still, it was something for her to be wary of.

When she returned to the cabin, she noticed a pizza box on the coffee table by the fireplace.

At least he wasn't still eating stale sandwiches. She continued to stay out of his way, and hurried up to her bedroom like a good little B&B hostess, wanting to give him nothing to complain about. And she also looked forward to continuing the Rip Tarrington thriller that she'd started over dinner. It was a gripping story, but to her surprise, Rip had a wry, tongue-in-cheek humor to many of his thoughts and words, that made the book fun to read. She could scarcely put it down when the time came to leave the diner.

Now, she entered her bedroom and froze. On her pillow was a single white carnation. There were no carnations growing near the cabin. In fact, the only one she ever saw near here was on Elijah Donnelly's lapel.

Could Alex have put it there? A peace offering, maybe? Somehow, she just didn't see it. But if not him, who? And whoever did it had been in the cabin … in her bedroom.

She picked up the carnation and as she drew it toward her, a light scent reached her. Lifting the flower to her nose, she knew she had smelled that flowery scent before. In the great room, in the kitchen. And now it filled her bedroom. But where earlier it had been soft, pleasant, and almost nonexistent, it now grew increasingly heavy, thick, and cloying.

Her lungs began to ache as the air turned thick and pungent. She couldn't breathe. She opened the window and flung the flower as hard as she could into the backyard, hoping the wind might catch it and blow it far away.

Then she slowly dropped down to sit on the floor by the open window, hoping the fresh air, the ability to breathe again, would calm her and bring her some explanation as to what had just happened.

But it didn't.

A loud crash jarred Carly awake. *What in the world?*

She sat up in bed. Hitchcock's barking told her she hadn't imagined the noise. She reached for her watch: 3:45.

Was it Alex? Had he fallen? Springing out of bed, she tossed her bathrobe over her arm and ran into the hallway.

The door at the other end of the hall flew open and Hitchcock bolted out, barking and running down the stairs. Alex quickly followed, but stopped at the sight of Carly. And stared.

So did she. The night was warm, and he wore pajama bottoms, no top, and she immediately saw that he was more muscular and well-toned than she had suspected. She had on thin nylon shorty pajamas. She quickly shrugged on her robe.

"I thought it might be you downstairs," he whispered. "Taking a tumble or something."

"And I thought it was you," she murmured. Hitchcock was no longer barking, but his low growl was scary. "Maybe we should call the sheriff."

"I'm not about to cower up here." He started forward.

"Wait." She caught his arm. His flesh felt warm. And muscular. And manly. Somehow, she found her voice. "If someone is down there, he knows we're awake by now. It could be dangerous."

"Wait here." Alex hurried down the stairs in the dark.

Holding the banister tight, Carly quietly followed. He motioned for her to stay back.

Hitchcock stood completely still at the entrance to the great room, a low growl continuing from deep in his throat.

Alex flipped the switch that turned on the lamps. "No one's here," he soon called.

Carly hurried into the room and saw that Elijah Donnelly's portrait had fallen off the wall. It seemed to have knocked some pewter pieces from the mantle, and the brass fireplace set's shovel, brush, and poker were strewn over the hearth.

The portrait itself lay face down on the hardwood floor.

"Oh, no," Carly murmured.

With the lights on, Hitchcock had stopped growling.

"No wonder we heard such a loud crash," Alex said, looking at everything that lay scattered. He picked up the portrait and studied the frame. "I don't see any damage. This frame is heavy, so no wonder it caused so many other things to fall."

Carly studied the spot where the portrait had hung. "But why did it fall? The picture hooks are still nailed in. Two of them." She reached up and tugged at them. They were solidly anchored to the wall.

"The wire's got to be loose, or something." He put the frame on the coffee table, face down, then tugged at the wire and the screws on the back. They appeared well fastened. He frowned as his gaze met hers. "As you said, what caused it to fall?"

He flipped the portrait over so that both of them stared Elijah Donnelly in the face.

The carnation that had been in his lapel was gone, and Carly's whole world went tipsy.

"Carly! Carly, talk to me. Here, sit down."

She found Alex holding her arms, helping her to the sofa. "Bend forward," he ordered. "Lower your head."

She did as told and soon the world became solid again. "What happened?" she asked as she slowly sat up.

"I was going to ask you that," he said. "You nearly fainted when I showed you the portrait."

He had put it on the floor to help her but picked it up now and placed it, face up, on the coffee table.

She drew in her breath a little too sharply.

"There's something about this portrait, isn't there? Something different," Alex said. "I could have sworn he was wearing boutonniere or something. But how can it be gone?"

"I don't think he was," she murmured, knowing she was lying. "And I'm fine now. Let's forget it."

He looked from her to the portrait. "I could be wrong, but I tell you—"

"Sometimes, the light in this room casts odd shadows or shimmers of light. I'm sure that's all it was," she said, far too sharply. "And I probably just got upset with all this late-night excitement. That could cause a person to feel faint, right? So, let's get old Elijah Donnelly back where he belongs so we can go to bed." That didn't come out right. "I mean—"

"Did you say Donnelly?" he asked.

His tone surprised her. "Yes."

Alex frowned. "Who is he?"

"Elijah Donnelly. He built the cabin. Why?"

"Just curious. Is he a relative? A great-great-grandfather or something?"

"At most he's some degree of uncle. His only son, Lucas, passed the cabin to my great-grandfather."

Alex studied her a long moment, then seemed to scan the room, his expression curious but also wary. What, she wondered, was going on with him? "So this must be the old Donnelly cabin." His voice was hushed.

She all but froze at those words. She forced a lilt to her voice. "I don't know that it has a name as such. Why? Did … did you hear something about the Donnelly cabin?"

His eyes narrowed a moment, but then he shook his head. "It's nothing. Just a name I once heard."

And exactly what, Carly wondered, had he heard about the name? Her eyes went to the portrait, and as she glanced at Elijah, a feeling stronger and stranger than ever struck her. Elijah's lips usually wore a slight smile, but now they looked more like a smirk. A smirk aimed at her.

Nonsense! Her childhood years of being scared of the cabin's "ghosts" were playing havoc with her now. She got up and walked to the hearth, her back to Alex and the portrait, as she placed the fireplace set back on the stone hearth and then stood without moving, trying to steady her mind, her being. "I suspect the picture fell because one of the workers who was here took it down and then didn't attach it back on the hangers properly," she said. "It might have been, literally, hanging by a thread."

"But why would it fall now?" he asked.

"Earthquake?" Carly suggested.

Alex got up on the hearth, ready to place the painting back on the wall. Carly grasped the bottom of the frame to steady it while he made sure the wire was properly attached to the hanger hardware.

"I think one of us would have felt an earthquake," Alex murmured as they both stepped back from the wall. The portrait listed slightly.

Alex shifted it a bit, then backed up, this time shoulder-to-shoulder with Carly as he eyed it again. It now hung perfectly straight.

Carly pulled her robe a little tighter around her neckline, unsure if her sudden quiver had to do with Elijah Donnelly's portrait or the closeness of the man beside her.

"Well, that was entertaining," she said brusquely, turning toward the foyer. "I wonder if I'll be able to go back to sleep tonight."

Alex grinned. "Probably." He then did a double-take as he looked from her to the portrait.

He stepped close to her, this time staring into her eyes. And as earlier, she found his nearness too ... well, she wasn't sure what it was. But she forced herself to remember how odious he could be.

She started to turn away from him, but he took hold of her wrist. "Did you know that you and the fellow in the portrait have the same color eyes?" he asked.

Her entire back stiffened, her nerves thrumming hard. She pulled her wrist free. "Nonsense. Mine are gray. No one has purple eyes. No one. I'm sure Elijah's eyes were blue. I suspect that his son mixed in a little lavender into the eye color as artistic license as he painted the portrait. And I assure you, my gray eyes don't change color."

"Usually your eyes are gray, but at other times ..." He shook his head as if confused as he looked from her to the portrait.

"I told you, the lighting in this room is odd."

"I was trained to be a careful observer. At one point, lives depended on it. I know what I saw, Carly, and I will get to the bottom of it."

"It's late," she announced. "I'm going back to bed."

She marched past Alex and Hitchcock and then ran up the stairs.

CHAPTER 9

Carly hurried downstairs the next morning but her step slowed as she entered the great room. Nearing the fireplace, she raised her eyes bit by bit.

No!

Elijah Donnelly's carnation was back on his lapel.

The only logical explanation was that the entire episode with the falling picture and Elijah's missing carnation had been a nightmare—a realistic nightmare brought on from finding a carnation in her room. She had had nightmares in the past that, even after she woke up, she thought the dream had truly happened. But they were dreams. Nothing more.

Her doctor's warning came to mind. He said she might see things if she didn't rest, and so far, this visit to the cabin had been anything but restful.

Something drew her back to Elijah Donnelly's portrait. She remembered in her nightmare that it had knocked things off the mantle as it fell. She picked up one of the pewter pieces that had supposedly fallen. On its surface were scratches, the sort that could have happened by falling, for example, onto the rough stone hearth.

Her finger rubbed the stone. The scratches might be old, but she didn't think so.

She stared up at the portrait. "What are you doing to me?"

The thought struck that she'd just talked to a hundred-year-old oil painting as if it could hear and understand her. Just how crazy was this situation making her?

She stood up and marched to the kitchen. It was ridiculous of her to worry about ghostly nightmares when she had a very real-life problem: staying at the cabin. Somehow, she needed to convince Alex Townson that she should remain here. The time had come for Carly the Caterer to up her game from simple pancakes.

As she mixed a cranberry scone batter, she decided on a menu of scrambled eggs, bacon, fresh melon slices, berries, and yogurt. She even squeezed some oranges for juice. The oven beeped, telling her it had preheated, and she put in the scones to bake.

That done, she was surprised to find that Alex had entered the great room and was staring at Elijah Donnelly's portrait.

"Good morning," she said pleasantly. "You're up earlier than usual. Breakfast will be ready shortly."

"That's fine," he murmured. He then got up on the hearth and removed Elijah's painting.

"What are you doing?" She hurried to him. "Why did you take that down?"

He carried the painting to a window and studied it in bright sunlight, then, his expression harsh, said, "Okay, how did you do it?"

She didn't like his tone or his words. "Excuse me?"

"How did you put the carnation back into the portrait?"

She froze. How could he know about the carnation? It was *her* dream. *Her* nightmare. "What are you talking about?"

Alex's gaze jumped from her to the painting. "Do you see the carnation in Elijah Donnelly's lapel? Well, last night it wasn't there. I thought he'd had a boutonniere, but I wasn't positive. Now I am. First you see it, then you don't, and now it's back. In other words, this is the original portrait. The one last night—without the carnation—wasn't."

It took her a moment to understand what he was suggesting. "Just a darn minute! You think I switched the paintings? That there are two? No way!"

He raised his chin. "The only other explanation is that the carnation was painted over and then painted back in. But there's no sign that happened, so there must be two portraits. You had to have changed them."

"Me? Of course I didn't! Why would I?"

"Maybe because this is the 'haunted Donnelly cabin.' You knew I'd hear about it, and your little stunt with the index cards yesterday, then the portrait falling last night is to get me to believe it." His gaze hardened. "You may think you've finally found a way to get rid of a tenant you don't want, but I don't scare that easily."

Her heart pounded so hard it was like a drumbeat in her ears; her entire body seemed to pulse with fury and distress. "I didn't! I'm as confused and troubled by all this as you are. Think about it! How could I have done what you're suggesting?"

He shook his head. "You must have had help."

She flung her arms heavenward, and all but shrieked, "Are you listening to yourself? Help? Who? Someone hiding in the attic? Oh, wait. There is no attic! And no basement. It's a cabin, remember? And I came here to be alone. And more than anything, right now, I wish I was alone!"

He studied her closely, and as he did, the tight contours around his mouth, the rigidity of his shoulders, the confusion that had emanated from him as he accused her, slowly vanished. Finally, he shut his eyes and in a soft voice said, "I hear what you're saying, but if not you, who would do it? And why?"

She hesitated for a long moment, but then blurted out, "I need to tell you ..."

He lifted an eyebrow. "Yes?"

She bit her bottom lip as she gathered strength. Finally, she sat down on the sofa. "I've been under a lot of stress about my business, and my doctor said I might—at times—imagine things, possibly even see things that ... that might not be there. But now, after what happened last night, I can't help but wonder ..."

"Go on," he all but whispered.

She felt almost desperate, her voice hushed. "What if the stress is causing me to *do* things that I don't remember as well?"

He looked honestly surprised. "Things like switching two similar paintings?"

"Perhaps. Except that I swear I don't remember ever hearing that there are two paintings!"

He sat down beside her, his eyes worried. "You've nearly passed out a couple of times. Is that because of the stress you're under?"

She wished she knew. "Probably. My doctor was unhappy with my blood pressure. I think it can cause faintness."

"I'd imagine." His mouth downturned. "I'm sorry to hear you're going through all that. I had no idea your job is causing you so much trouble."

She nodded. "It's crazy, I know."

"No. Not at all." He carried the portrait to the mantle and rehung it. "But there's still the issue of where that second portrait might be—the one without the carnation. And, I'd like to know if there's someone besides you involved in all this."

"You don't think it was me who switched the portraits?" she asked.

"Somehow, I just can't imagine that," he admitted. "After breakfast, you and I are going to search the cabin and the grounds around it for that other portrait. Once we find it, it'll give us a good idea of what's going on here and who's trying to gaslight us. Don't worry. We'll fix this."

"Okay, then, after breakfast.... Oh no! Breakfast!" She dashed to the oven and took out the scones. They looked like blackened lumps of coal.

After breakfast sans scones, Alex said it was time to go on a hunt for a second painting.

Carly shook her head. "I'm sure there's no second painting. And anyway, aren't you supposed to be working on your book?"

"I am," he admitted. "But how can I concentrate with all this weirdness going on? I need answers. Only then I can work without any distractions."

"I'm sure no one is sneaking around in here," Carly said.

He raised his eyebrows. "Oh? Are you saying you're the one switching the paintings? You do know that isn't normal behavior."

She clutched her hair. "So now you think I'm crazy! I never should have told you what my doctor said."

"You're definitely not crazy," he said calmly. "But if not you, who's doing these strange things? Just what is going on here?"

"Maybe someone is trying to scare *you* away," she said.

"But I didn't tell anyone I was here. No one except my agent. And the last thing he wants is to distract me from writing. Which means, the only person I know who wants me gone from here is you."

"Back to square one," she muttered.

"Exactly. So we've got to search this house for either the portrait, or some means of entry that you aren't aware of."

Finally, she relented. They started upstairs and worked their way through the house, searching every closet, nook and cranny for a spot where a portrait might be hidden. They found nothing.

They went into the garage filled with Alex's Mercedes, rusted tools, and two ancient lawn mowers.

"Here are some old boxes," Alex called from the back of the garage.

She joined him to see two fairly large boxes stacked in a corner.

Alex opened the top one. Inside, was a large, folded piece of crochet work. When Carly tried to lift a portion of it, several of its delicate threads tore in her hands. She then carefully scooped up the entire piece and removed it from the box. "It's so large it must have been a tablecloth," she said. "I wonder which of my relatives knew how to crochet with such a fine thread. This must have taken years to make. I'm sure it was once quite beautiful."

"Probably so," Alex murmured as he rummaged through the rest of the box. She had the impression he had no idea what crochet was or how difficult it was to do well. "Seems to be nothing but tablecloths and napkins and such. Everything looks old, faded, and probably not worth saving."

"I don't know about that," Carly mused. If there was some way to save the tablecloth, she definitely would.

Alex opened the second box. It was filled with what looked like automobile parts. Carly wouldn't have been surprised to learn they were from a Model T.

They continued to hunt through the garage, but found nothing more.

"This was a waste," Alex said, disappointed.

"Don't worry, Sherlock," Carly said. "You'll deduce what's going on. I have confidence."

"Thank you, Watson."

Back in the cabin, Alex sat down at his computer while Carly made herself a cup of coffee and went up to her bedroom to study her business books. When she reached the door, she hesitated, then pushed it open.

No carnation or any other thing lay on her pillow, or anywhere else in the room. She checked. Including under the bed.

Finally, she stretched out on the bed, her coffee on the nightstand, and opened *Business Expansion for Dummies*.

She read, fighting sleep because of her miserable sleep the night before, but she was determined to get her books read.

The next thing she knew, she heard a light tap on her bedroom door.

She opened her eyes to discover she had turned onto her side, a pillow scrunched under her head, and the book she'd been reading was not only shut, but upside down.

Her watch read 7:10. She couldn't believe it. She opened the door to find Alex grinning at her. "You look like you've been asleep. I thought you were working."

"I was," she said, then frowned. "And discovered that business books are a cure for insomnia."

"Ah, readings to deal with your business troubles."

"So the book jackets claimed," she said with a frown.

He lightly smiled then put his hand on the doorjamb. "Well, I don't feel like another pizza. The TV dinner in the fridge looks even less appealing, so I'm headed to Crouch to find a restaurant. Want to join me?"

His suggestion surprised her. He was actually being pleasant, and frankly, if she were being honest, she'd have to admit he'd been quite reasonable throughout this decidedly unpleasant experience. How could she not go with him? She smiled. "Absolutely."

CHAPTER 10

Mama's Folly, a restaurant, bar, and dance floor, had been in business for years. Its wooden walls were filled with posters of old Western movies, photos of cowboy actors, and hanging paraphernalia ranging from cowbells to stirrups, bridles, and antlers. The best thing that could be said about Mama's Folly was that it was a step up from the Rusty Nail where Carly had eaten the night before. Mama's also had a live country-western band. It was crowded when Alex and Carly arrived, but they found a table.

They surprised each other by both ordering chicken-fried steak and mashed potatoes smothered in country gravy.

"I suggested we come here because Mama's chicken fried steak was famous when I was a kid," Carly said. "I hope it's still as good as it used to be." Dining at Mama's wasn't exactly the reason she had decided to change into a nice dress and had ditched the pony-tail to wear her long hair down—but it would do for the moment.

Alex looked around the restaurant, then met her gaze with a smile. The place was jumping, and when the band started playing "(I've Got) Friends in Low Places," it was met with a rousing cheer. "Judging from the number of people here on Monday night, I suspect the food is as good as ever."

Carly returned his smile as the waitress brought them each a draft beer. She kept glancing his way. Like her, he'd changed into nicer clothes and was looking quite handsome.

"So tell me," Alex began, "what brought you to the cabin at this time?"

She tucked a strand of hair behind her ear as she pondered how much she should tell him. "I simply needed to get away for a while."

When she said nothing more, he asked, "Because of the stress from your job?"

She nodded.

"But if that's the case, shouldn't you be trying to put business issues out of your mind? Why are you reading those aid-to-insomnia business books?"

She frowned. In for a penny... "Well, if you must know, the stress has come about because I don't know what to do about my business. I'm hoping I can figure it out while I'm here."

He looked impressed. "So you have your own business?"

"I do. I'm a caterer which is why it's nothing for me to prepare a meal for you." Her words were matter-of-fact. "I'm used to creating spreads for a hundred or more. Cooking at the cabin is child's play."

"So you really do know cooking. I thought you were just joking around, but that explains why your food is so good. Have you always loved cooking?" he asked.

She hesitated, but since she was being honest, she said, "I don't know that I ever loved it." He was the first person she'd ever admitted that to. Maybe because he was the first who'd bothered to ask. Still, she hurried to explain. "But my father did, you see. He started the business, and I took it over when he passed away. He even named it for me."

"I'm sorry to hear he's gone," Alex said, his eyes concerned and watching her closely.

"Thank you. He's been gone quite a while, but I still miss him so much. He was a good man, and a great dad." She paused a moment and was about to say more when their dinners were served.

Carly looked over at the dancers. She couldn't remember the last time she'd gone to a club with dancing. She couldn't help but smile and tap her toes as people did a lively country two-step to "Play Something Country." It was the sort of song she never, ever heard in San Francisco.

They soon picked up the conversation while enjoying the meal.

"So, if I'm understanding," he said, "although you aren't crazy about catering, you're obviously a very good cook, and you want to make your business bigger and better."

"At this point, I'll be happy with profitable."

His brows rose. "Well, that's practical."

"I hope so. It turns out my college major wasn't the smartest choice. At least this way, I'm working."

"What was your major?"

"Botany."

He showed no emotion on his face. "As in plants?"

She grinned. "I'm glad you didn't laugh the way most people do."

"Not at all. It's actually an interesting choice." He filled his fork with meat, potato, and gravy, and seemed to savor the taste a moment before asking, "What made you choose botany?"

"I love flowers." At his puzzled look, she smiled. "I was always told to study what I love, and I foolishly believed the advice. Then I learned that to do botanical research or even to teach, a person needs a Ph.D. But my dad got sick before I even earned my bachelor's."

"Do you ever think of going back to school?"

She shook her head and pushed around the gravy before replying, "Not when there's no time or money. But if I did, I'd probably try for a certificate in horticulture or landscape design."

"Why is that?"

She couldn't get over how interested he seemed, and how many questions he asked. No one else, not her mother or her sisters, had questioned her this way. "I worked one summer at a nursery," she said, her voice wistful at the memories that summer brought her. "I loved it. The huge variety of flowers and shrubs, helping people figure out the best plants for their particular location and soil type, and watching the incredible beauty and complexity of nature at its finest was a glorious way to make a living. Learning about plant structure, how to nurture them, and help them grow healthier and stronger, was exciting. Especially orchids. I adore orchids. They're truly unique and incredible flowers. I used to dream of running my own nursery, but opening one in San Francisco would be impossible. Not only are the rents there ridiculously high, but people aren't exactly waiting with bated breath for a new nursery to open."

"What about a flower shop?" Alex asked.

She shook her head. "In San Francisco, they're either huge and expensive enough to cover the rent, or they're franchises in which the floral displays are prearranged and sold on a website. Nothing particularly creative or interesting is going on there."

"So why stay in San Francisco?"

"It's always been home. And my catering business is there."

His eyebrows rose. "So, Ms. Carly Fullerton, if you could open a nursery anywhere in the world, where would it be?"

She was game. "Ruling out London, Paris, Rome, and places like that?"

He nodded. "For now."

"I haven't thought about it that seriously," she admitted. "Although frankly, a place around here, in or near Boise, would work well. It's one of the fastest growing areas in the country, and new homes need landscaping."

"That's true," he said, but then his mouth formed a mischievous grin. "But it must feel strange that now, instead of growing plants for beauty and pleasure, you cook them."

"Oooh, that hurts!" She wrinkled her nose. "I prefer to think of it as using plants, in whatever form, to give pleasure."

He chuckled, but then his gaze turned sympathetic. "I can see from your eyes, the way they sparkle when you speak of flowers and botany—you have a very expressive face, by the way, and beautiful eyes—that catering doesn't excite you the way they do."

She gave a dejected sigh. "It doesn't, but I do like being my own boss. And I like my customers. And … and thank you." Her cheeks grew warm at his unexpected compliment.

The band began a rousing, window-shaking version of "Boot Stompin' Boogie," and more people than usual were getting up to join the line dance.

When the dancing switched to swing with "Sweet Home Alabama," Alex faced at her. "It looks like people are having fun. How about it?"

Her jaw dropped. Surely he was joking. "I didn't think writers from Boston danced in country-western bars."

"There's a first time for everything," he said. "I'll just consider it research."

It had been a few years since she'd danced and it was on the tip of her tongue to turn him down. But he was watching the dancers with a smile. She guessed she could handle one dance. "In that case, let's do it."

He danced a nice swing, and to her surprise, she was having fun dancing. They were both grinning broadly when the song ended. The lead singer then insisted everyone stay on the dance floor for "Achy Breaky Heart,"—especially anyone who'd never line danced before.

Alex nearly walked off the floor, but Carly stopped him. "Come on, you've got to try this."

"You know how to line dance?" He sounded surprised.

"Of course. My sister, Julia, taught us. And she was the toughest instructor I've ever had, so believe me, I still know how to do it."

"Well I don't."

"Think of it as research," she said with a devious smile.

He looked more than a little horrified, but then nodded.

She kept him by her side, talking him through the steps as the lead singer called them out, and before long, Alex was laughing at his mistakes and from the smile on his face, she saw that he was having a good time. To her surprise, so was she.

The dance no sooner ended than the singer said, "Grab your partner," and began "When You Say Nothing at All," a slow tune.

Alex faced her. "I'm so used to following that guy's orders, I can't stop now." He then took Carly in his arms. His build was rangy, but she could feel his strength as he held her. She was tall, but he was taller. She placed a hand on his broad shoulder and it was as if she'd been hit by a jolt at the feel of his muscles under her fingertips and the heat radiating off him.

She swallowed hard with the realization that she liked the firmness of his hands on her, and the way his closeness made her feel. This wasn't, she reminded herself, a date, but he was certainly enjoyable to be with. And slow dancing with him had awakened feelings that long lay dormant. Feelings she needed to quickly set aside.

When the song was over, the band took a break.

She turned away from him and pushed her hair back off her shoulders, breathing deeply a moment before facing him again. "It's probably time for us to head home," she said, more than a little befuddled by her reaction to their dance. She needed to get her emotions back to being strictly professional. She quickly led the way back to their table to pay the bill and get their things.

"I'm paying half." Carly dug into her handbag for her wallet as the waitress came by with their check.

"I don't think so." Alex handed the woman his credit card.

Carly was about to object when a voice said, "Carly? Carly Fullerton? Is that really you?"

She turned to see who knew her name. Blond hair. Tanned complexion. Broad shoulders. And large, very pale blue eyes. He was giving her a cautious, curious half-smile. Suddenly she remembered a skinny little boy full of mischievousness and fun. "Gunnar! Oh, my goodness! Can it be?"

"It sure is," he said.

"I can't believe it!" She gave him a quick hug. "So good to see you!"

"You, too. How ever are you?" he asked, his thin face stretched tight in an ear-to-ear grin. "And what in the world are you doing back in these parts?"

She turned to Alex. "This is an old friend, Gunnar McDermott. Gunnar, this is my houseguest, Alex Townson."

The two shook hands. Obviously, Carly thought, like her, Gunnar didn't recognize Alex's name or his books.

"House guest?" Gunnar asked her, looking with more than a little curiosity at the two of them. Carly also noticed that Alex gave Gunnar an equally curious once-over, his eyes jumping from her to Gunnar and back again.

Carly quickly explained to Gunnar about her mother's death and turning the cabin into a B&B.

"I'm truly sorry about your mama," Gunnar said. "But does this mean you'll be around here a whole lot more?"

"I'm not sure, but Julia will be."

He cringed and hooked a thumb in the side pocket of his jeans. "I still remember how your big sister used to do a right-eous job of twisting my ear when she got mad at me for no good reason that I could ever tell."

Carly laughed. "That was Julia, all right. And still is, I'm afraid."

"Your little sister was sweet, though," he added.

"Mallory still is the most easy-going of the three of us," Carly admitted. "And often, too sweet for her own good, I'm sorry to say."

"Sweetness is a virtue, nonetheless," Gunnar said with determination.

"Perhaps. But tell me about yourself," Carly said. "What have you been up to?"

"Not much." His words were clipped, as if he didn't want to talk about it. She noticed an odd look passed between him and Alex, and then she saw the cane on his far side.

"Are you married or anything?" she asked.

"No." His gaze dropped a moment. "Never was so lucky. Kind of slim pickings around Garden Valley, I guess."

"I guess," Carly said.

"You?"

"No, me neither. Same with my sisters."

He was taken aback. "That's sure surprising, considering..." He censored what he almost said. But Carly knew. Roxanne's many marriages and the fact that her three daughters had three different fathers were the talk of Garden Valley over the many summers Roxanne and the girls had visited. Now, Gunnar and Carly met each other's eyes, and both laughed.

Alex looked completely baffled by them.

"Such is life," Carly said.

"So it is," Gunnar agreed. "Although your mama, she could sing like an angel."

"Yes, that she could," Carly said.

Just then, the waitress returned with Alex's credit card and receipt. Time to go.

"It was great seeing you," Carly said to Gunnar. "I'm staying out at the cabin, possibly for another two weeks. Drop by if you have time, and we can catch up."

"I'd like that," Gunnar said with a slight tip of the head. He glanced at Alex. "Good to meet you."

"Same here, soldier," Alex said.

Gunnar froze a moment, then straightened, held Alex's eye and gave a crisp nod. "You, too." Carly watched him use the cane as he left the restaurant.

CHAPTER 11

As Alex observed Carly in the kitchen the next morning, he now understood why she was so fast and efficient and why her cooking was such a joy to eat. But her health issues caused by her troubles with the state of her business troubled him. He hoped she could find a way to relax here at the cabin. He had enjoyed watching her have fun last evening at Mama's Folly—enjoyed it a bit too much, truth be told. He had to concentrate on his book, not on his hostess. But now, he caught her eye and then patted his stomach. "I was never one for breakfast, but I love yours."

"I do make my living cooking." She gave him a small smile, her large gray eyes surprisingly wistful. He stared at them, and it struck him like a bolt that he loved looking into her eyes.

He wasn't sure how to handle that. He thought back to her statement, and realized that, from her tone, talk of cooking made her unhappy. Not, of course, that it should matter how he talked around her. She'd be gone in a week and a half, after all.

He was sorry about that. Obviously, he was more starved for companionship than he had realized. And for fun. It had been a long, long time since he'd enjoyed himself as much as he had last night.

"But I don't hate cooking," she added as she wiped down the counter. "Not at all. And preparing meals for two is far more enjoyable than doing a large spread for a mass of strangers. Some of those wedding parties are killers."

He forced his thoughts back to what she was saying rather than to the woman herself. "I can't imagine doing anything like that."

She pointed at his index cards. "And I can't imagine taking all those notes and making anything either coherent or exciting, let alone both, out of them."

Alex wished she hadn't reminded him. He gazed at the cards and heaved a sigh. "Sometimes, I can't either." He got off the counter stool and walked over to the dining table that now served as his desk. "I suppose it's time for me to get to work. That book won't write itself."

She folded up the dishtowel. "And I've got to study my business books."

He remained standing as he watched her walk over to the stairs. She had said she would disappear when she wasn't cooking for him, and she was doing as she promised. Strangely, he didn't want her to go. And he definitely didn't feel like staring at a blank computer screen again.

Hitchcock trotted past her to the front door and barked, then pulled his leash off the small table in the foyer and faced Alex expectantly. Bless you, Hitch.

"I think someone is telling me he wants to go for a walk," Alex said. "It's not right to keep him cooped up. He's probably stir crazy."

"I can take him," she offered, "if you'd like to work on your book."

"The exercise will do me good after that meal," he said, but when he glanced at her, words that surprised even him fell from his lips. "If you have the time, why not join us? And maybe you know an easy way down to the river that you could show me."

A smile slowly brightened her face. "I could, couldn't I?"

The June sun was warm in the Idaho mountains, the sky bright blue, and the air crisp. As Carly, Alex, and Hitchcock left the cabin, a family of chukars ran across the road and into the brush. The little ones looking wobbly on their feet and Carly wondered if they could fly yet.

As they neared the water, they saw mallards and wood ducks. Carly enjoyed the look of pleasure on Alex's face as he watched them glide along the river.

"This is paradise," he said, taking in the scenery. "And so peaceful."

"It is, but if you follow our river downstream until it merges with the main stem of the Payette, you'll see quite a different river. Larger and faster. It's wide and deep enough for white-water rafting."

"Really? I'd love to see it," Alex said, then faced her. "How about it?"

She was stunned. "Now?"

"If you have time."

Business books versus the beauty of nature; being with Alex versus being cooped up in her bedroom. "I certainly do."

They took Carly's compact Toyota so Alex could take in the sights. Hitchcock filled the entire backseat. Carly drove along the middle fork to the south fork of the Payette River through steep, rocky mountains until it met with the river's main stem at the tiny town of Banks. There she parked.

The two, with Hitchcock, hiked through trees and brush and scrambled over rocks to reach the river, and then continued along its bank. As promised, the river was wide, fast, and cold.

Carly had done no climbing like that since she was a teenager, while Alex appeared to be completely at home on rugged terrain and was having the time of his life.

Several times a group of rafters floated by and waved merrily at them and their huge dog.

Carly was also thrilled that she remembered so much about the surrounding flora from her college classes. Once again, Alex seemed genuinely attentive as she told him about the different marsh plants.

Eventually, the bank became too steep to safely climb. Alex stepped as close as he dared to the water's edge and held out his hand for Carly to join him. She did, and they sat with their feet dangling above the water. Alex was quiet, as she was, the silence interrupted only by the faint lapping of the water against the rocks, the call of a dove, or the songs of a marsh wren or thrush.

This silence, this peace, was what had been missing in her life. She was completely enjoying the day, and the man at her side, quiet, attentive, at times funny, yet clearly attuned to the beauty of nature around them, struck her as the perfect companion to enjoy it with. The thought jarred her, and even more jarring was the recognition that being out here with him caused her heart opened to him. Only slightly, yet it was enough to both surprise and terrify her.

The last thing she needed in her life at the moment was the complexity and challenge and disappointment that went along with falling for anyone. She'd had very few boyfriends in her life, and never one she was very serious about, but she'd watched love destroy people. Good people, like her father. And some that were maybe not so good ... like her mother. In any case, she'd been careful to steer clear of anyone who could turn her life into such a muddle. Now, finding this stranger so inter-esting and enjoyable to be around went against the extreme caution she normally held. What, she wondered, was going on with her?

At the same time, although they had talked a lot, she knew little about him, as if there was a part of himself he walled off. She remembered reading his bio, that he had been a counterintelligence agent in the Army. She wondered if that caused his air of mystery, or if something more was going on.

He didn't talk at all about his life back in Boston. She respected that and took care not to come right out and ask him about it. She gave him plenty of openings in case he wanted to talk. But he didn't. For all she knew, he could be married, or engaged, or even be the Boston Strangler.

She also couldn't help but notice, as they scrambled along the banks of the Payette, that he constantly looked out for her, and helped her around bushes and over rocks. With him, she felt safe. The realization was comforting, although she had no idea why that should be. And there was no reason at all for her to dwell on these many aspects of him. After all, he would soon be back in Boston with a new book out. He'd be lauded and feted, while she would be making tiny triangle sandwiches in a hot commercial kitchen in San Francisco.

At that moment, the gentle breeze seemed to turn chilly, and they soon headed back to the cabin.

When they returned to Crouch, they wandered into its one antique shop, as if both were loath to return to the tasks awaiting them. Hitchcock got lots of attention in the store and out of it. He had to wait in the car, however, as they made a quick stop at the grocers for Carly to buy porterhouse steaks, Idaho potatoes, all the trimmings for bakers, and a combination of greens for a salad. After two days of other people's dinners, she was looking forward to cooking one of her own.

"I feel as if I've spent the entire day playing hooky," Carly said with a laugh as they returned to the cabin.

"That's because we have," Alex said, grinning as he followed her inside. But then his gaze turned serious. "And I enjoyed every minute of it."

Her pulse skipped a beat. She felt as if some strange spirit had come over her … or over Alex … making the man she once found detestable turn into someone warm and charming.

Alex had bought a margarita mix and tequila at the state liquor store and made them each a margarita over ice as a before-dinner drink. After having them and relaxing on the porch, Carly went into the house to put on dinner.

Before long, they sat and ate. Alex took a bite of the meat, and then some baked potato with all the typical Idaho trimmings of cheese, bacon, chive, butter, and sour cream. He shut his eyes for a moment. "I have to say, the restaurants were fine, but this dinner is outstanding."

After dinner they had coffee outdoors. Although she had read a biography of Alex on the Internet, she felt awkward about him knowing it. So, she asked, "Have you always been a writer?"

"Not at all. After high school, I joined the Army. I didn't want anything to do with books or reading, and definitely not writing. But the Army changed all that."

"Really? How?"

He leaned back against the pillow-covered park-like bench they sat on. "I guess it happened when I learned about Military Intelligence. And no jokes about that being an oxymoron, okay? There really is such a thing, and it's great. From the time I first saw those guys at work, I wanted in. But that meant I had to go to college, so I did. And eventually, I got into the unit."

"Did it live up to what you expected?"

"More than. I loved every minute of it."

"What kind of things did you like?"

"Well, if I told you"—he grinned—"you know what comes next."

"Curtains for me."

He chuckled and nodded. "Life is tough sometimes."

"Great!" she smirked.

He then turned the conversation to war movies he'd known and loved. She knew a couple of them, but romantic comedies were her favorites. She didn't talk to him about them.

The sun shone until nearly ten at night in Idaho in early summer, so it was fairly late before the sky turned dark and they decided to retire for the night.

As Carly walked through the great room, she felt the strange eyes of Elijah Donnelly on her.

CHAPTER 12

The rat-a-tat of morning rain sounded on the cabin's roof and against the bedroom windows.

It was the kind of day made for lounging in bed, but Carly had a guest to feed and her own business to think about.

After returning from the restaurant, she went up to her bedroom, picked up his story on her e-book reader, and couldn't stop reading until she'd finished the book. She loved Rip Tarrington, a complex character who was fun but also had a loving, serious side that made her root for him. She marveled at Alex's talent and writing ability.

A little sleepy that morning from lack of sleep, she went downstairs to set up breakfast. The cabin was quiet, and she guessed she wasn't the only one who'd stayed awake too late last night.

She decided to take a moment to sit quietly and give thought to her catering business. She needed an idea that excited her. If she wasn't excited about her business, how could she expect strangers to be? She needed an idea that inspired her, that offered joy and fun to customers. She sat by the fireplace, telling herself to come up with a way to cater with enthusiasm.

And to stop thinking about her lodger.

She glanced up at Elijah's portrait. He was again smirking at her.

So much for thoughts of her business!

She got up and headed for the kitchen area to start breakfast, but as she passed the dining table, her eye caught Alex's index cards, now in small rubber-banded, color-coded bundles, and she remembered how they'd flown about the room.

As she stepped closer to them, her eye caught the words "Tajikistan history." Tajikistan? She'd never heard of it.

She picked up the bundle and was soon reading about Marco Polo's journey across the Central Asia area, of its endless wars, and how the small tribal land eventually fell under the rule of Russian Tsars. Once they were overthrown, it became one of many ethnic areas that had made up the USSR, one of the Soviet Social Republics. When the USSR broke apart, Tajikistan established its own government.

"Well, well. Are my cards that interesting?"

She spun around at Alex's voice, and couldn't stop a smile as she looked at him. He had a warm, just-awakened look. He wore a robe and hadn't combed his hair. The unshaven look he was sporting was growing more obvious by the day.

"I came down to get a cup of coffee," he said, "but I found myself standing here for a while watching you. You seemed quite engrossed."

Her cheeks reddened. "I was. I didn't mean to spy or anything, but I found myself curious about Tajikistan, and started reading. Sorry." She quickly put the rubber band back on the cards.

"It's quite all right," he said.

She started breakfast, although Alex looked good enough to

be the main course. The thought caused her cheeks to redden even more than they were already.

"You're up earlier than usual," she said, trying to sound casual as she turned on the burner under a frying pan and placed crumbled pork sausage in it. "I'll have an omelet on the table in no time."

He came over to her. "No rush," he said. "But it surely smells good." He placed his hand on her shoulder a brief moment before he turned away to pour himself a cup of coffee.

She all but dropped the spatula at his touch. It was as if she'd been hit with an electric shock.

"So, what did you think of Tajikistan's history?" He sat at the counter and took a sip of coffee.

"It's a fascinating place. I never even knew it existed." She spun away to the refrigerator. She grabbed the orange juice, poured them each a glass, and then put them on the island near their seats. She hated all the inner turmoil he caused her, and could only hope he hadn't noticed. It had been a long time since a man had caused her to feel so discombobulated.

"Neither do most people." He shook his head. "I'm glad to hear there's something about this story that might be intriguing."

"Have you ever been there?" she asked.

"No, but I met a few guys who had been. But as a military intel analyst, I met all kinds of interesting people. That's where I learned a lot of the spy stuff I use in my books."

"It all sounds quite exciting," she said wistfully, as she dished out their omelets with toasted English muffins and marmalade.

"Have you traveled much?" he asked.

They sat side-by-side at the counter. "Never left the U.S. I'd love to, but my business keeps me much too busy for that. And too broke."

"I'm sorry to hear it."

"But tell me more about you." She cocked her head, her eyes

curious. "You called your military job fascinating, but you left it. Was it to write?"

He looked chagrined. "I left to get a law degree."

"That seems like quite a change."

"Too much of one," he said. "I left law as well. Guess I'm not a paragon of stability, am I?"

She frowned. "Or, you're willing to take chances, to go where life leads you and see what happens. I admire that."

"You're being kind."

"Actually, I'm jealous," she said. "It's better than getting burned out doing something you don't love."

"Perhaps," he murmured. "But it has its own drawbacks, especially when you hit a roadblock like I have with this latest book. I'm getting nowhere."

"Maybe you're putting too much pressure on yourself. And trust me, I know all about pressure. So after you've finished the breakfast I made for you, you're going to write up a storm."

"You're cooking your way into staying at the cabin, are you?" he teased.

Something made her give a saucy toss of the head and reply, "I am, indeed."

"You're a regular Scheherazade, but you ply me with food instead of stories." He chuckled as he poured them both another cup of coffee. "I can't say I object. It's surprising, but I even find I'm sleeping better than ever."

She smiled. "Fresh air and sunshine will do that to you."

"It's more than that. Despite a few odd moments, I'm finding that being here—the cabin, the river, the company—to be relaxing and peaceful. I can't help but think coming here was exactly what I needed."

"What company? We haven't had—"

"You."

Her breath caught. She felt she should joke at his words, to toss some riposte back at him, but then she decided to enjoy and be heartened by his words. "You aren't such bad company your-self," she said softly.

Their breakfast finished, she started to clean up the kitchen while Alex moved to his computer.

Alex had enjoyed his time at Mama's Folly so much last evening, he was tempted to ask Carly if she wanted to go again that night. But he immediately had second and third thoughts and realized that wouldn't be a smart thing to do. He found her far too interesting, and far too attractive. He didn't come all this way to get into a romantic entanglement with his bed and breakfast owner, for pity's sake! For all he knew, she had a steady boyfriend in San Francisco. He'd never asked, and she'd never said. Besides, he had a book to write.

As dinnertime approached, he returned, alone, to the Rusty Nail.

Just as he had the first time he went there, he started out at the bar.

"Welcome, back," Butch said, wiping off the bar in front of Alex, then putting down a coaster. "What can I do for you?"

"Whiskey and water."

As Butch poured, he asked, "Are you enjoying our little town?"

"I am," Alex said. "And, it turns out I'm staying at the old Donnelly cabin."

Butch's bushy eyebrows rose up. "You are? What do you think?"

"Some weird things go on there, all right. But it's not ghosts. I think someone is trying to mess with the owner of it. I know she shares ownership with her two sisters, and from what she's said, the only thing I can come up with—so far, at least—is that one or both are hoping to get her to sell her share by scaring her away."

"Is that so?" Butch said.

"Have you ever heard anything about bad blood between the sisters, or maybe others in the family? She doesn't say much about them."

Butch rubbed the end of his mustache. "No, can't say that. I do remember the mother, though. She was a firecracker, that one! Used to spend time at the cabin each summer when her daughters were little. But one year, she didn't come back. That was that, and the place stayed empty until just recently."

"So you don't know anything about other possible owners?" Alex asked.

"I don't, but someone who might is the town's realtor, Emma Hughes. Her office is on the main street heading out to the Banks-Lowman Road."

"Thanks," Alex said. "And right now, I could go for one of your burgers. The one I had the other night was incredible."

"I can send one to a table, or would you like to see the menu?"

"I'll go with a sure winner. Thanks." Alex took his drink and moved to a table.

Alex's mind was filled with thoughts about the "ghostly" cabin as he ate dinner. When he returned to the cabin some forty-five minutes later, he noticed an old cassette tape player and a small box of cassettes sitting on the antique credenza against a far wall. It hadn't been there before.

He went over to it and found that the tapes were labeled with names of songs from old Broadway musicals. He was surprised by how many of them he recognized.

He remembered hearing that Carly's mother could "sing like an angel." He wondered if she might have made these tapes.

He turned on the cassette player, chose a tape, and put it on. The sound of a woman singing "Till There Was You," from *The*

Music Man, filled the room. Whoever she was, her voice was beautiful.

He sat on the sofa to listen.

Carly came rushing in. She looked pale. "What's going on here?"

"What do you mean?"

Her gaze focused on the cassette player and the box beside it. "Where did you find those?"

"There were here when I came in," Alex said. "I assumed you put it there. Who's singing? I love her voice."

"Roxanne Donnelly." Her voice quavered. She sat on an easy chair then quietly added, "My mother. I didn't know any recordings of her existed."

"There's a bunch in that box."

The shock on her face had to be real, he thought. No one could be that good an actress. She went to the tapes to look through them. "I remember her practicing these," she whispered.

"She sounds like a pro," Alex added.

"She was. She toured in musicals. Off-Broadway musicals."

"She sounds good enough to me to be on Broadway."

"From all I've heard," Carly said as she continued through the tapes, "there was always someone just a little better—a voice a little stronger, a range a little wider. But she was doing what she loved. And a lot of the younger performers didn't know the old songs, which were her forte. They were into *Miss Saigon, Phantom, Les Mis*—things like that, which Roxanne never bothered to learn. In that sense, she was her own worst enemy."

"But her name is Roxanne Donnelly, not Fullerton?" he asked.

Carly's stomach sank. She hated talking about her mother. "My father wasn't her only husband—not by a long shot. And being a singer and in theater, Roxanne stuck with her maiden name." Carly backed away from the tapes and their strange, sudden appearance. "I probably should go back upstairs and let you get to work. Do you want to let this continue, or would you like me to shut it off?"

"Actually, those songs about love just might help me get into the emotion Rip Tarrington needs."

Just then, Roxanne's voice singing "*I'm gonna love one man 'til I die,*" drifted over the room.

"See what I mean about her singing old songs?" Carly forced a lilt to her voice. "That one is nearly a hundred years old. It's from *Show Boat.*"

"*Show Boat,* yes! In fact …" Alex said and pulled open the bottom drawer of the credenza. "Look."

Carly followed and peered down into the drawer's contents. "I remember those CDs," she murmured. "My mother brought them to the cabin years ago. I can't believe she just left them here."

"I discovered them a couple nights ago," Alex said. "They're older, lots are musicals, and listening to them didn't interest me at the time. But *Show Boat* is a great, and now I'm in the mood to hear all of it. Ah! Here it is."

He turned on the CD player and placed the disc on its platter.

As the first song began, he said, "Feel free to stick around if you want." He tried to sound casual, but he could hear the hope in his tone.

With a slight nod, she sat on the sofa. He was glad she joined him and couldn't help but wonder if she, like he, had "an old soul." Soon, he found himself lost in the hardships of "Old Man River," and the hopefulness of "Make Believe (I Love You)." Looking at her expression, it seemed she felt the same.

CHAPTER 13

The next morning after breakfast, while Alex was out on the deck with his coffee and a couple of magazines he'd bought in Crouch, Carly took the opportunity to use the dining room table before Alex sat down to work at it.

Using slow, cautious movements, she carefully unfolded the crocheted tablecloth she'd found in the garage so she could see how large it was, but more importantly, to see how much of the crochet work needed repair and if it would be possible to mend.

The cloth was much larger than she had imagined. As she neared the last few folds, she saw a paper between them. She had no idea why it was there. Perhaps it would give the name of the crocheter. Maybe even the year it was made.

The last fold of the tablecloth revealed a lot of damage. Carly shook her head. To repair it would be beyond her ability, and would take more time than she had. Still, she couldn't imagine throwing it away. She would talk to Julia and Mallory, although she was sure neither of them knew which end of a crochet hook to use.

Her gaze returned to the paper, now in the center of the table. It had been folded into a small rectangle, and it took a few turns to open it up. But when she finished, she stared in astonishment.

She then ran to the French doors and flung them open. "Alex, come quick! You've got to see this."

Alex put down his coffee cup and magazine and entered the great room. "What's going on?"

"It's a letter. It was tucked inside the tablecloth. The ink has faded, but it's still legible. Look!" She handed it to him.

August 8, 1923

My dear Theodore,

I have little time left in this world. For that reason, I am writing to tell you that I have willed my cabin to you in hopes it shall thereby remain in our family. Fear it not, for despite unnerving rumors you may have heard, I can attest that it has brought me nothing but great comfort. It is my refuge from the world, and it is my fondest hope that it shall be yours as well.

And if, by chance, when you know you are alone in it, you see movement or a strange form pass by, do not be afraid. If my prayers are answered, I shall soon be with them, among the shadows, forever.

Your cousin,

Lucas Donnelly

"Wait. Lucas Donnelly?" Alex asked, handing her back the letter. "Elijah's son?"

"Yes! The one who painted the portrait. Look at the date."

"He said he's dying," Alex said. "I wonder how old he was then."

"Not very," Carly said. "I'd say thirty-two at the most. We think the cabin was built around 1890. Oh, my, let me think. Roxanne used to tell us about the family. As I recall, soon after Elijah built the house, his wife, Lucas's mother, died in childbirth and Elijah died within a year or so. It's said of a broken heart, but who knows? Anyway, Lucas was sent to live with relatives, and when he was old enough, he joined the Army. Then, when the U.S. entered World War I, he was sent to fight, and apparently, was never the same after that. When he returned, he came to live in the cabin, essentially as a hermit."

"If he was dying in 1923," Alex said, "it could have been from damage caused by the mustard gas in the war, or even something like TB."

"I always had the impression he had what they used to call 'shell shock,' which I guess is the old term for PTSD. But all I've ever heard is what my mother told me, so we should take it with a grain of salt."

"At least you know the cousin's name, Theodore. You can look him up."

"I don't have to. He was my mother's grandfather. And he was the one who started the legend about the ghosts."

Alex's brows furrowed. "And you think it was because of what Lucas implied in the letter?"

"More than implied. Look at his words: 'if … you see movement or a strange form passed by' and 'I shall soon be among them.' Theodore swore Lucas and his parents haunt this cabin. Now, we know why Theodore believed that. Lucas told him."

"But Lucas was a dying man when he wrote this, so who knows what his physical and mental state was," Alex said.

"True, but the way Roxanne told it, her grandfather, Grandpa Teddy, had been a shy and lonely man. Lucas gave him the cabin because he saw Theodore as a kindred spirit, doomed to a life of loneliness."

Alex's eyebrows rose. "Obviously, since Theodore is your great-grandfather, that isn't the way it turned out."

"Right. Theodore was living here, alone, and one day a pretty woman knocked on the door. She'd been riding and her horse stepped in a hole or something and came up lame.

She saw smoke from the cabin and came here looking for help. She and Theodore ended up getting married. They built more rooms onto the cabin and lived here with their children. Theodore told everyone who would listen that he did not have a fire burning in the cabin that day, so there would have been no way for his wife to have seen any smoke. He swore the ghosts of the cabin were the ones who brought his wife to him. He also said he'd seen the ghosts in the house, but he didn't mind them. After all, they'd brought him true love."

"Sounds weird," Alex said. "Matchmaking ghosts."

Carly gave him an amused glance. "Anyway, everyone thought Theodore and his wife were a little batty, living out here all by themselves, ghosts or not. They had three children, and their middle child, a son, was a loner just like his father had been. When the parents got too old to live out in the woods alone, they gave the cabin to that son, making him promise he'd never sell it."

"And obviously, he met someone to love, since your mother was born," Alex said.

"Not really. While my great uncle Paul was living here, alone, a woman who was part of a group rafting on the river got into trouble and they beached the raft. The cabin was the closest building, so they went to it. The woman fell hard for Paul. But for whatever reason, they never married. And he never met anyone else. After a few years, he left, and gave the cabin to his younger sister. It's said when he died, he was alone and bitter and cursed the cabin for having ruined his life. Roxanne believed the woman also never found anyone else to love, and she also died alone."

"Strange," Alex said.

"Yes. That brought up the part of the story that says if the ghosts get two people together in the cabin and it doesn't work out, those people are doomed to a loveless life."

"Based on what happened to that one relative?" Alex said skeptically.

"Why not? Anyway, Paul gave the cabin to my great aunt Edith, a spinster, as they used to be called. She was here only a few months when she met a man from England who was traveling through the area because the American West intrigued him. He had heard stories about the cabin, and one day knocked on the door, and there she was. She was in her forties at the time, and never thought she'd find anyone to love, but she did. She and the Englishman married, and went back to England, and I never heard what happened to either of them."

Alex shook his head, eyebrows high. "That's remarkable."

"Isn't it? I mean, Idaho is such a young state, no stories go back many generations, but those are interesting, I think. Anyway, Roxanne's father, Douglas, ended up with the cabin after his sister left the country. He was already happily married and came up here just for vacations. Grandpa Douglas worked on the cabin, too. I remember him and Grandma Betty well. They were always nice to me. Anyway, since Roxanne was his only child, she inherited it from him. He made her swear she would never sell it. Amazingly, she listened to him."

"Did she make the same request of her daughters?"

"Actually, she didn't make any request of us. She pretty much ignored the cabin for the last fifteen years of her life. And ignored her daughters, as well. I hadn't spoken to her in several years and hadn't been told she was sick."

"That's terrible," he said.

"I suppose," Carly murmured. "But then she never came to see my dad, who'd been her second husband, when he was dying and didn't go to his funeral. She wasn't there at all for me through what was the most difficult time of my life. Maybe I'm a bad person, but I couldn't forgive her for that."

"I notice you often call her 'Roxanne' instead of 'my mother,'" Alex said. "I can't help but suspect she was a very unhappy person."

Carly grimaced. "She definitely wasn't filled with joy where her daughters were concerned. But enough about her. All I know is, Grandpa Douglas was sure his brother, Paul, never married because of the curse of the ghosts. He didn't marry the woman the ghosts found for him, and he lived alone and lonely as a result. He was also sure his sister, Edith, met her future husband because of the ghosts. Roxanne grew up with these stories and passed them on to my sisters and me."

"The stories sound barmy, you know," Alex told her with a smile.

"I guess. But Grandpa Douglas also believed he saw the ghosts, and Roxanne thought she had as well. Believe me, those stories were scary but also thrilling for us kids."

"Looking at Roxanne," Alex said, "she must have found what she thought was true love many times but it sounds as if she may have died alone and lonely."

"I suspect she did. But she never met any of her husbands at the cabin," Carly said. "Maybe that was her problem."

Alex looked at her skeptically. "So you're saying the ghosts may have found a true love for her and she ignored him, just like her uncle Paul ignored his true love? And she ended up cursed?"

Carly almost took him seriously—she had wondered exactly that, in fact—but then she saw the gleam in his eyes. "Obviously, you've solved the puzzle. I'm afraid, however, that Roxanne never talked of meeting anyone at the cabin and if you ask me, her first and maybe her only love was her musical career."

Alex nodded. "That makes the most sense. In fact, it amazes me that anyone ever met a prospective spouse at a place as remote as this cabin. I mean, the whole idea is ridiculous."

"It is. Of course, you and I met at the cabin ..." The words were no sooner out of her mouth than she wished she could take them back.

"Uh, oh!" His eyebrows rose. "But, actually, that was more the fault of your sister, Julia, than any ghosts."

She gave a tense little chuckle. "Saved by Julia! Okay. I can live with that."

He chuckled as well, but she detected a slight nervousness to the sound. He cleared his throat. "Anyway, to me, the biggest surprise is that Roxanne didn't sell the place," Alex said. "She seems like someone who would value cash in hand more than old family stories."

"She used to tell us girls that she remembered how much she enjoyed spending time in the cabin as a child, and that was the reason she would bring my sisters and me here each summer when we were kids. She used to tell us the cabin was magical. A place where true love waits. She swore it either helped, or it hurt, and a person never knew which it would be."

Alex nodded thoughtfully, then sat down with his laptop. Time for work.

Carly carefully folded up the tablecloth and Lucas Donnelly's letter. She had quite a story to tell her sisters.

CHAPTER 14

By the following day, Carly had decided she'd been mistaken to think that anything more than friendship had developed between her and Alex—at least not on Alex's part. Especially after finding Lucas Donnelly's letter the prior afternoon, she thought they might have dinner together and talk more about what it all meant. But he didn't ask her to join him, and since she swore she wouldn't disturb him, she kept her word, difficult though it was.

When she went into town to buy fresh fruit for the next morning's breakfast and some chicken to cook for her dinner that night, she also stopped at a coffee shop with internet service, and downloaded Alex's second book onto her e-reader.

Interestingly, as much as she liked Rip Tarrington, he was nothing like the man who created him. Rip was a bit of a stud, quick to fight, quicker to argue, and blundered his way through life like a bull in a china shop. And quite the lady's man. Women threw themselves at him, and they shared wild nights of mad, passionate ecstasy. She couldn't help but suspect Rip was a typical male fantasy.

Rip was also the anti-Alex. Where Alex was cautious,

thoughtful, and studious, and probably analyzed everything to death before making a decision—she could see why he had been in Army Intelligence—Rip rarely thought before he acted. Tough, loud, outspoken, and ready to fight at the drop of a hat, he was also surprisingly funny.

Rip's humor was a side Carly hadn't seen much of in Alex. But clearly, it was there.

She loved a man with a nice sense of humor.

A couple of days passed in which breakfast became the highlight of Carly's day. At breakfast, she and Alex fell into an easy early morning banter as Carly cooked something scrumptious and filling for them both—she quickly noticed that he never bothered to eat lunch—and they talked about their work and any plans for the day, which were always to continue what they'd started the day before. But it was a comfortable time, especially since she could tell by Alex's expression, as well as the fact that breakfast seemed to go on for longer and longer each day, that he enjoyed their time together as much as she did.

After that, she would go off to her room, or into Crouch, or take a walk alone or with Hitchcock. The only "bad" thing was, instead of reading business books, she was reading Rip Tarrington's adventures. She'd now finished book two and was into book three.

On Friday evening, Alex knocked on the door and asked if she'd like to share the pizza he was ordering for dinner.

They put the pizza along with some beer on the coffee table and Alex went over to the CDs. "Would you like some music?" he asked Carly.

"Sure, if you don't mind a choice between show tunes and show tunes."

He smiled at her quip, and she found herself liking that he enjoyed her poor excuse for jokes, and that he seemed to enjoy being with her. "I guess you know them all," he mused.

"Absolutely. Roxanne loved to sing them for the family, and pretty much anyone else who would listen."

"That must have been great."

"Except that people kept thinking I should be able to sing—as if such talent could be inherited." Carly shook her head remembering those times. "I can barely carry a tune. Mallory's voice is okay, and I don't think I've ever heard Julia sing even 'Happy Birthday.' When other kids knew songs from Beyonce and Eminem, I could recite every line from every song in *My Fair Lady.*"

"Ha! More power to you, in my opinion."

She frowned. "You wouldn't say that if you'd lived it. But I didn't see Roxanne often, so it didn't matter all that much."

"Thank goodness she didn't sing disco," Alex deadpanned, still going through the CDs.

That made Carly laugh out loud. Alex gave her a smile as if her laughter pleased him. And that was something else she liked about him—very much.

Somehow one of the CDs fell out of the group Alex was flipping through and onto his foot.

"What's this?" he said, picking it up. "I'm not familiar with this musical. *Carousel.* Is it one you like?"

"I love it. In fact, Richard Rodgers said it was the favorite of all his musicals. But it can be sad in parts."

He grinned. "I promise I won't cry." He put it on and then sat down to read the insert that explained the story and the songs.

As he read, she listened to the music. Before long, one of her mother's favorite songs played, "If I Loved You." Carly had forgotten how much she used to enjoy hearing Roxanne sing the sad and plaintive love song, a song about a woman so afraid to confess how she feels that the person she loves goes away, never knowing how she felt.

"There's something quite romantic about the song, isn't there?" he asked, studying her face.

She hoped he didn't notice how completely absorbed she had been listening to it. She had never told a man she loved him; never had a reason to. "Be careful," she said softly when she found her voice again. "You don't want the cabin's ghosts to turn you into a romantic. What would Rip Tarrington do then?"

"Poor Rip. Good point. I can't let the ghosts or the cabin enchant him into a sense of peace and contentment. Heaven forbid!"

"Well, keep in mind that things don't always turn out happily for those who stay here."

Green eyes, frowning and serious, captured hers. "Do you believe in the cabin's magic?"

She drew in her breath. "No. Of course not."

He fell silent until the song came to an end.

"Beautiful," Alex whispered, his gaze meeting hers.

Carly's breath caught as the word seemed to have a double meaning. "It is," she murmured.

He poured them some wine and then sat beside her. As they listened to the rest of the album, his presence warmed her and filled the solitary cabin in a way that made her feel safe and secure.

"We'll have to listen to more of these old musicals," Alex said when the CD ended. "I've heard some of these songs, but I didn't know the context."

Carly nodded. She never admitted it to anyone but, having grown up with these old tunes and a mother who performed in musicals, they made up nearly all her favorite songs. It amazed her to meet a man who could also enjoy them.

Not that she would ever tell him that. It wasn't anything he needed to know as she reminded herself for the umpteenth time that no matter how much she enjoyed his company—his jokes, his laughter, even the way he chewed his pencil as he stared at comments and notes he'd jot in the margins of his computer printouts—that no matter how much he made her temperature rise that he was her B&B guest. Nothing more. She would be going back to the West Coast soon, and two weeks after she left, he would return to the East Coast … "and never the twain shall meet."

She soon said good night and headed up to her bedroom.

She knew she couldn't handle many more evenings like this one. She had enjoyed being with him far too much.

CHAPTER 15

Alex was trying his best to work on his novel and to ignore Carly Fullerton and the Donnelly ghosts, but nothing was working the way he'd planned or hoped. First, it was impossible to be oblivious to Carly unless he were dead. He had no idea why she appealed to him as much as she did, but the more he tried to disregard her, the more he wanted to be with her to the point where he had put on old show tunes that he didn't even know simply to watch her face light up.

He wrote lots of words, but at the end of the day, when he'd reread what he'd written, the DELETE key became his friend. The story was awful. There was no way he could send it to his agent.

And then there was the Donnelly ghost issue. His latest suspicion was that somebody was messing with him because that morning, when he opened his novel to Chapter One whose contents he had deleted the previous evening, he saw the words, "Good Morning."

The computer was password protected, and he simply didn't see Carly as a hacker.

So who could have done such a thing?

For that reason, after breakfast, when she went up to her bedroom to work on her business plans or whatever she did all day, he drove to the office of Emma Hughes, realtor.

The office was in what had once been a single family home on the main road to Crouch. It looked like it was at least sixty or seventy years old, with a front porch and clapboard siding. The sign proclaimed it to be a realty office and insurance company. A bell chimed as he went in the door, and an attractive young woman came out of a back room to greet him.

"Hello. I'm Emma Hughes, can I help you?"

"My name is Alex Townson. I'm not actually here to do business, but I'm hoping you can give me some information."

"Please have a seat and tell me what this is about." She stepped behind the desk and gestured for him to take one of the chairs facing it.

He explained that he was staying at the Donnelly cabin, now a bed and breakfast, but that strange things were happening there, and he was curious about its history.

She folded her hands. "All I know is that it's been in the same family for generations. Everyone thought it had been abandoned until late last year when it was renovated."

He nodded. "I know all that. I'm wondering about … about the ghosts."

She scoffed. "Silly rumors, nothing more. I think they came about because the cabin looked spooky when no one took care of it. But beyond that, there's nothing I can tell you."

"That makes sense." He drew in his breath. "I understand that when the last owner died, her daughters inherited it, fixed it up, and made it into a B&B. Have you ever heard anything about other relatives wanting it? Or, maybe, trouble between the three sisters as to who should own it?"

She shook her head. "I don't think anyone else wants it. Land simply isn't worth much out this way. We've got plenty of it, all undeveloped. And an old cabin doesn't add much value. In fact, most people were surprised to hear anyone was spending money to fix it up."

What she said made sense. "But, strange things …"

The look she gave him told him if he didn't keep his mouth shut, she might call the sheriff and he'd end up in a rubber room. "Okay," he said, standing. "I'm glad you clarified all that for me. Power of suggestion can be strong." He chuckled. "Sorry to have bothered you."

She stood as well. "No bother at all. But if that old place isn't to your liking, I've got plenty of beautiful, new cabins for rent. I'm sure one of them will be perfect for you."

"I'll keep that in mind. Thanks."

He got out of there as fast as he could. He was going to have to figure this out on his own.

On Saturday, Carly realized her first week at the cabin had ended. She hated the thought, but knew she had to return to her city, her business, at the end of next week although she still hadn't come up with a plan to make her business more profitable.

One problem was that she wasn't all that dedicated to studying the business books she'd brought.

It was bad enough that as soon as she finished one of Alex's books, she would make a quick trip down to Crouch to get Wi-Fi service to download the next book in the series. She also spent far too much time thinking about Alex and their conversations. And listening to old musicals with him showed her a different side, a sentimental side, that she found quite charming in a man.

As the afternoon wore on, she felt hungry. She glanced at the clock and saw it was nearly six. She didn't feel like cooking, and decided she would go to Crouch—alone, as usual—to get something to eat.

She was about to leave her room when she heard a voice, a man's voice. *"You like him. Let him know it."*

"What? Who?" She spun around to see who was talking to her.

No one was there. It didn't sound like Alex's voice, and she couldn't think of anyone else who might be talking to her. Was Alex playing some kind of joke?

"You can look pretty, you know."

She dropped onto the bed. She couldn't tell which direction the voice came from, almost as if she were hearing her own thoughts.

The idea made her nervous, both because she didn't know the voice, but also because the words she heard were true. She did like him. And with a little effort, as Roxanne once told her, she could look attractive.

A movement caught the corner of her eye and she turned her head to see the closet door slowly opening.

Carly scrambled up onto the bed. A rat, she told herself. A big, outdoors rat. Or a raccoon. Or who knows what might have found its way into the room and was now pushing open the door.

But the door stopped moving, and no critter appeared.

Her heart pounding, she tiptoed to the closet. Nothing was there.

Then, a group of hangers suddenly zipped to the left, revealing one of her prettiest tops. Form fitting, it was a soft jersey material with a deep V-neckline in a kelly green color that beautifully set off her red hair.

Carly's heart pounded as she looked from side to side. She was alone in the room. But something made her reach for the top. She went to a mirror and held it against her.

Yes!

She unfastened the clip that held her hair up, brushed it out, and then put on eyeliner, mascara, and lipstick. Next, she changed into a short black skirt, the kelly green top, and strappy, black, high-heeled shoes. She almost hadn't brought any dressy clothes with her, but at the last minute decided to.

"I'm being silly," she told herself. "And the closet door didn't really open all by itself. I did it without really thinking about what I was doing. Nothing more."

Yet, having spent many summers in the cabin, she'd learned to pay attention to "feelings" about things she needed to do. And when the feelings turned to hearing words and seeing movement, she knew she had to follow instructions.

Realistically, however, it could also mean she had gone stark raving mad.

She had no plan for dinner, only the strange sense that she should try to convince Alex to join her. But if he didn't, she'd go out alone. She looked at the ceiling and slowly turned in a circle as she said, "What do you think about that, Elijah? Or is that what your plan is? Maybe someone else is out there for me. Someone who isn't Alex Townson."

Actually, she hoped there was, because Boston's Alex Townson, big-time author, certainly wasn't the type to be interested in a stressed-out, money-losing, ghost-believing caterer.

She left her bedroom and started down the stairs.

At the same moment, Alex stepped into the foyer and looked up at her. He wore a sports jacket and dress slacks. She stopped on the stairs. His eyes brightened and his face warmed in a smile. "I'm wondering if you'd like to go someplace special for dinner tonight." But he no sooner said that, than his expression changed to a frown. "Although ... the way you're dressed. You look beautiful, by the way. But do you already have plans? Maybe with Gunnar or—"

"Not at all." Was he jealous? No, impossible. In fact, she

hadn't heard from Gunnar, nor did she expect to. "It's Saturday night, and I felt like going out."

He looked downcast. "Oh."

"Actually, I was hoping you might want to join me."

"Really?" His expression softened, and he moved closer, resting a hand atop the newel of the banister as his green eyes captured hers. "For some reason, I had the sudden urge to dress nice, even to put on a tie. And here we are."

Her heart was thumping. "Yes, here we are."

His eyebrows lifted. "Let me assure you of one thing. It was my idea to be with you. Not some ghost's."

She wondered what made him say that. Had he heard suggestions to dress up and ask her out—in his own mind but not quite—the way she had? Maybe the ghosts were at work here, but if so, they were only urging what she already wanted to do, giving her encouragement to act, and she could only hope it was the same for him. In fact, she couldn't imagine anyone or anything, including ghosts, forcing Alex Townson to do anything he didn't really want to. She made no comment, but smiled in a way that said, "I understand."

"Tonight," he said as he reached for her hand while she walked down the last few steps, "I want to be with you, to go to dinner, and for us to remember that there's more to life than writing my book or worrying about your business. Other things, like people, are also important."

His words were exactly what she was hoping to hear and they matched her own thoughts exactly. "That's true," she whispered.

"You might"—he brushed a lock of hair back from her face, and his fingertips lingered on her cheek, his voice husky—"meet someone. Someone you want to spend time getting to know ..."

She could scarcely breathe at his words, his expression, his gentle touch. *Yes,* she wanted to say. *Yes, yes.*

He let his hands drop and backed up a step as if realizing

how intimate his words had become. He took a moment to smooth his jacket. "Anyway, I had the idea, I know it's probably a waste of time, but what if we went out and found a nice restaurant somewhere beyond Crouch? We might even go into Boise. It's only an hour or so away." He stopped himself, as if fearing he had said too much.

Not nearly enough, her heart said. "That's a great idea," she said. "I heard people in Crouch mention a new restaurant in Horseshoe Bend right on the Payette River. I haven't tried it, so it might be awful, but the location is wonderful."

"Let's try it," he said, then grinned, "but if it looks or smells like a greasy spoon, we keep going."

She chuckled. "It's a deal."

He placed his hand on her waist and escorted her out the door. "And I wasn't just spouting words earlier. You really do look beautiful tonight."

"Thank you," she murmured, beyond pleased.

But as they walked to his car, she couldn't stop her gaze from turning back to the cabin, and she said a silent "thank you."

CHAPTER 16

Alex kept driving until he found a restaurant that fit, as he said, "the way they were dressed." But Carly couldn't help but hope he was feeling, as she was, that something had changed in their relationship that night, and they were both ready to acknowledge it with a special meal.

They found that in a small French restaurant in a town called Eagle that sat on the edge of the foothills before Boise. With its dim lights, intimate setting, and soft French music in the background, it was everything Carly had hoped they would find.

"So tell me, Mr. Thriller Writer," Carly said as their entrees, beef bourguignon for him, bouillabaisse for her, arrived and both began to eat, "what do you do when you aren't enmeshed in writing a novel?"

"Well, the thing I'm happiest about is supporting a place called the Gilbertson Foundation. It's a group home for boys."

"Really?" That wasn't at all what she expected to hear. "That sounds quite nice. How did you get involved in it?"

"I had a really good friend when I was in the Army. He was a mentor to me, took me under his wing and taught me the ropes

—he's now a major, by the way—and it was the orphanage where he grew up, the place he kept being sent back to when foster homes didn't work out for him. The people there taught him to straighten up and study hard. It led him to the Army where he's one of the best guys and the bravest man I've ever met."

"That's surprising," she said. "I'd always heard foster homes were better for kids than orphanages."

"They usually are. But a bad foster home is much worse than a group home, which is the term used these days instead of 'orphanage' because a lot of the kids aren't orphans, but were abandoned or given up by their parents. Also, group homes are now heavily regulated so the abuses you sometimes heard about are very rare. But, to your point, some kids simply don't do well in foster care. Some are, frankly, too willful, and even too big and strong for foster parents to handle. Those kids are sent back to a group home."

"I had no idea."

He nodded. "Most people don't. Particularly with older kids, teenagers, they're much more likely to run away from a foster home and end up living on the streets than to run from a group home where their movements are much more regulated and restricted. Not that restricting them is great, but living on the street is even worse."

"I can imagine," she said, surprised by how much information he had about the issue. It was also clear how much helping those boys meant to him.

"In fact," he said with a wry smile, "I can attribute my success at writing to the Gilbertson Foundation."

"Oh?"

"When I saw how difficult it was for the people running it to keep it going due to money issues, I wanted to help them. I've always been interested in writing, in being a writer, and I'd been playing around with an angst-filled literary book for years and getting nowhere. One day, I realized that if I could write a popular book, I just might be able to make some money and help them out."

She had finished her bouillabaisse and took a sip of Chablis. "It was that easy?"

"In a way. It was almost a lark. But I kept thinking about my time in the service, and out of the blue came the idea of writing a thriller based on some situations I'd investigated, some neat places I'd traveled to or had learned about—like Tajikistan—and a lot of the really wild stories I'd heard. I came up with a tough, larger-than-life figure who was everything I'd never be. Somehow it worked because a top agent, Jack Bellar, took me on. Jack sold my first Rip Tarrington thriller. People liked Rip and wanted to read more about him. I donated a lot of the money from that book to the Gilbertson Foundation, and the rest, as they say, is history."

"Wow," she said with a smile. "So you deciding to do a good deed led to great success."

His face suddenly changed completely from the smile he wore to one much more serious, even despondent. He pushed aside the last couple of bites of his bourguignon and reached for his wine glass. "Actually, there's a lot more to it. And a lot that isn't nearly as noble as you just made it sound. But let's say, yes, we did help each other out, fortunately."

The waiter appeared just then. "May I offer you some dessert?"

Alex looked at Carly. "Your call," he said.

"I'm sure it'd be wonderful," she said, "but I have no room for any."

Alex nodded. "I'm the same."

"Ready to go?" he asked Carly with a smile after paying for their dinner. She noticed that they were the last two diners. She hadn't realized they had sat and talked for so long.

She nodded, glad to see that whatever had caused his brief,

troubling reaction to her comment had passed.

It was approaching eleven o'clock when they returned to the cabin feeling happy and content. As they walked into the great room, Carly suspected she should say good night and go up to her room. "Well ..." she began.

"How about some wine?" he quickly asked, his face bright and hopeful.

Her heart leaped. Maybe he also didn't want the evening to end. "I'd love some," she said breathlessly. But then prudence made her add, "Although I don't want to keep you if you think you should get back to work. I know you like to work late into the night."

"Can I help it," Alex cocked his head slightly as if taking in every contour of her face, "if I don't want the evening to end yet?"

How was it that he always said the right thing? "I don't either," she admitted.

"I know you also have things you should be doing," he said as he went into the pantry and found a bottle of wine.

"Do I?" Her smile broadened as she removed her jacket and remained by the sofa. "I don't remember."

"Good." He placed the wine on the kitchen island without stopping as he headed back to her. Their gazes met and, as he approached, the desire in his eyes warmed her. "I must admit," he added, "working on my book is the last thing on my mind right now."

She smiled at his words and stepped toward him. She wanted this, wanted him.

But then Hitchcock let out a deep, rolling bark, followed by the distinct sound of a car door slamming.

They froze.

Hitchcock was at the window beside the front door, barking excitedly.

Alex looked worried. "Who could be coming here this late?"

"I'll find out," Carly said. Trying to get her heartbeat to return to normal, she headed toward the door.

"Wait," Alex warned as he grabbed Hitchcock's collar and pulled him away from the window. "You don't know—"

Carly swung the door open. A blond woman wearing a pale pink pants suit faced her. Her eyes swept over Carly from head to toe.

"Can I help you?" Carly asked.

"I'm looking for Alex Townson."

Carly gaped at her. Why was she looking for Alex? Who was she?

Thoughts, unkind thoughts, swirled through Carly's head as she zeroed in on the woman before her, ticking off her faults. The woman's hair—too light to be her natural color—was long and straight. Probably extensions. Dark eyeshadow framed her eyes along with a wide swath of liner and fake eyelashes so long and thick they probably caused a breeze when she blinked. Her mouth had the pouty look of someone who'd added collagen to her lips, and even her cheekbones, to Carly's eye, were too high and apple-round.

Some people—men … Alex—probably found her attractive.

Alex stepped past Carly and glared at the newcomer. "What are you doing here?"

The woman nodded at the Uber driver, who then carried her two bags to the front door. Leaving the bags, the woman sauntered into the great room.

"Skye," Alex demanded, "answer the question."

"Isn't this charming," she muttered as one eyebrow lifted at the wine on the countertop. Then her gaze centered on Carly. "And who are you?"

"Carly Fullerton, I own this B&B."

"Ah! That's good news. I was so worried about my poor Alex being all alone in some remote middle-of-nowhere cabin that I thought I had better come and take care of him. But now I see he isn't living as monk-like as I'd imagined."

Carly's cheeks reddened as her gaze jumped from Alex to Skye. So that's how it was, Carly thought.

"Wait, Carly," Alex said. "It's not what you think."

She stiffened. All she wanted to do was run up to her room and put the pillow over her head. Instead, ever the perfect B&B hostess, she tightened her jaw against any expression or emotion as she stepped outside and wheeled Skye's suitcase and carry-on into the foyer and then shut the front door.

"Skye, what possessed you to come here?" she heard Alex say. "You need to leave."

Carly remained absolutely still and waited to hear Skye's answer.

"Leave? Why? Can't I stay with you?" Skye stepped close to him, placing her hands on his shoulders.

"We've been through this," he said through gritted teeth. He backed away from her. Her hands dropped to her sides. "There's nothing between us."

This wasn't at all the scene Carly expected. And apparently, not what Skye had expected either.

Skye's bottom lip jutted way out. The woman could pout, Carly thought. "I know you don't mean that. And anyway, I let my Uber driver go. He was quite unhappy at having to take me out this way. I saw Hitchcock at the window when I first arrived, so I knew you weren't far. I had him wait until we saw lights come on in the cabin. Apparently, there won't be any other drivers here until tomorrow morning."

"I'll take you to a hotel," Alex stated.

Skye spun around as if she knew Carly was still standing there taking it all in. "Surely, you wouldn't mind another guest here tonight, would you?"

Carly didn't know what to say. She glanced at Alex, but he had his back to them as he stared out the French doors, his arms folded. Just from the tense way he hunched his shoulders, Carly could see he was furious. "I … I do have a spare bedroom."

"Good. I'll take it." She smiled at Carly. "I'm sure Alex is simply surprised I'm here, and that's why he's so grumpy. He'll be better in the morning. And right now, I'm exhausted. I've been traveling since five a.m., Boston time. I had no idea any place in the U.S. could be so out-of-the-way. If you don't mind, I'd like to go to my room."

"Sure." Carly went to pick up the larger suitcase, but Alex grabbed it before she did, gave her a startling cold, hard look as he did so, and headed up the stairs. "Follow me," Carly said to Skye, leaving the carry-on for her.

Carly led Skye into the remaining bedroom after Alex left the suitcase and fled back downstairs without another glance her way. "This is yours."

Skye's mouth remained downturned as she looked over the plain, old-fashioned room, then faced Carly. "You must wonder about me showing up uninvited."

Carly did, but she wasn't about to admit it. "Not at all. Mr. Townson is a guest. I don't know anything about him or his personal life."

Skye lifted one eyebrow as if she didn't believe a word Carly had just said. "Oh, well, if that's the case, you're one of the few women who's spent time around Alex who hasn't fallen victim to those gorgeous green eyes, wavy hair, and great body. We had an argument a little while back, and I asked him for a cooling-off period. He gave it to me. But now that I'm cooled off, I'm here to take him back."

"I see." Carly's teeth gritted. "And you're sure he wants that?"

"I know he does," Skye said. "It all had to do with his ex-wife's marriage, as I guess you've heard."

"Ex-wife?" Carly blurted without thought.

She had suspected he might have been married, but now Skye confirmed it. Skye suddenly looked like the cat who ate the canary. "You don't know about his ex?"

"I don't gossip with my guests about their lives," Carly stated with as much dignity as she could muster.

Skye strolled around the room a moment before turning to face Carly. "Well, you should know he's extremely upset about it. That was the reason for our breakup and, I'm sure, for him running away to this no-man's-land."

"I see." Carly turned back the covers of the bed and fluffed the pillows. It felt good to hit something.

"Anyway," Skye continued, "I told him he needs to get over her. He doesn't like being told what to do, even when it's for his own good."

"Right."

"Thank you for your help," Skye said, clearly dismissing Carly.

Carly put the key to the bedroom on the dresser. "You can lock your room if you wish. Also, I'll be serving breakfast in the morning, but feel free to use the kitchen anytime. It's stocked with a variety of food and drink if you're hungry or thirsty. Just help yourself."

Skye said nothing.

"Goodnight," Carly said.

Skye gave a dismissive nod and turned to unzip her suitcase.

Carly paused at the top of the stairs. She should go downstairs and tell Alex his friend had settled in. But tonight, especially after the look he gave her, she couldn't be that gracious of a hostess.

She went to her bedroom and shut the door a little too forcefully.

CHAPTER 17

Carly was surprised when Skye joined her for coffee at 8:30 the next morning, but the woman immediately pointed out that in Boston, it was already 10:30, a civilized hour for a civilized place. And that was why she found herself awake at a time and in a place she clearly considered uncivilized.

Carly had planned to make Alex Eggs Benedict using her own recipe for English muffins and a from-scratch hollandaise sauce. Despite the newcomer, she went ahead with her plan. Since she had no idea when Alex would be up, she cooked Skye's breakfast right away. Looking at how rail thin Skye was, she was sure that one egg and half of an English muffin were the most the woman would ever eat.

"Eggs Benedict. Homemade," Carly proudly announced as she placed the food before Skye on the counter a while later.

Skye gaped in horror at the dish. "I can't eat that."

Carly stared at the plate. Was there a dead bug on it? A strand of hair? She saw nothing wrong. "You can't?"

Skye glowered at her. "It has Canadian bacon. I eat nothing

that once had a face. The muffin contains gluten. And I only eat egg whites, never yolks. They're just too disgusting."

The harsh smile on Carly's face all but morphed into a grimace. "I'm so sorry. I had no idea. What would you like?" Carly asked as pleasantly as she was able.

Skye shrugged. "If you have any fruit or vegetables, I could go for a smoothie."

"I can do that," Carly said.

She used the spinach she had intended for eggs Florentine in the smoothie, along with the tomato and avocado she had planned to use for guacamole to go with the margaritas Alex enjoyed. She cut everything up and blended it and then walked the glass over to Skye, who had moved over to the sofa. Skye took it without a word and then marched up to her bedroom, glass in hand.

About an hour later, Alex came downstairs.

Carly's eyes met his for only a second before she spun away, saying nothing, and prepared their breakfasts.

Alex ran his fingers through his hair and stood by the kitchen island. "Look, I'm sorry about this. I had no idea she'd show up."

"It's okay." Carly began to fry the Canadian bacon.

"No," he countered, stepping to her side. "It isn't. And last night—I almost overstepped. Or, perhaps I did. In any case, I was caught up in the moment, as if we'd been on a date. I'm sorry for that, too."

Hearing that, fury struck—at him, but most of all at herself. She put a coffee pod in the machine and pressed the start button, glad, for once, for its loud grinding and whirring. Caught up in the moment, was he? God, but she was a fool. She had no such excuses. She knew exactly how she felt. His words made her almost—*almost*—glad Skye had shown up and interrupted something that could have caused her to feel a lot worse.

The coffee made, she placed the mug in front of him. "No need to apologize. I may have also been a tiny bit 'caught up.'"

He nodded. "Glad that's settled."

"It was nothing. Nothing at all."

"As for Skye, I'll get her to leave today."

"No need," Carly said. "It appears you two had a spat, and now she's here to make up."

"It was nothing so dramatic." He sipped the hot brew. "I met her through my agent, and we dated. Three times, which was two too many. There was nothing between us, never would be, and I told her that."

Carly had the English muffins warming, the eggs poaching, and she was stirring the Hollandaise sauce hoping it wouldn't separate. Her breathing quickened as Skye's words about his ex-wife filled her mind. Skye might mean nothing to him, but obviously, his ex still did. That had to be why he never even mentioned having been married. She drew in her breath, needing to confront him, even as she feared what his answer might be. "She said you were upset about your ex-wife getting married again."

His lips tightened. "Well, you women certainly can cover a lot of territory in just a few minutes, can't you?"

She turned away from her cooking and spun toward him. "When it's important, Alex. And you're important to … to Skye."

He studied her, saying nothing a long moment. "When I learned my ex was going to remarry—the wedding was the Saturday I arrived here—it caused quite a bit of soul-searching. It made me think about what went wrong with the two of us, made me think about where I was going with my life, and what I wanted to do with it. And it made me think about the so-called relationships I was having. There were—I'm sorry to say—a number of women like Skye in my life since my divorce. Attractive, fun, shallow. Maybe that's not fair, but my ex is a lawyer, a brilliant lawyer. She doesn't have a shallow bone in her body.

Skye, and others, weren't what I was looking for. I tried to explain that to Skye. Obviously, she doesn't listen. If she had, she never would have come here."

Carly lifted her chin high. "She might have only paid attention to what she wanted to hear—the bit about your ex getting married again. And how much it upset you."

He shook his head. "No. She understood I didn't want to see her anymore."

"But you told her you were here."

"No way!" He looked defiant. "Her brother is a tech at Google. He can find out anything she wants about anyone. I'm sure he just looked at my credit card."

She dished out the Eggs Benedict and poured her perfect Hollandaise sauce over them and then walked around to the side of the counter with bar stools and placed the dishes atop placemats where the two of them normally sat. That explained Skye, but what about his ex-wife? Was he still in love with her, as Skye claimed? He hadn't said, only that his ex was brilliant, and an attorney. How, Carly wondered, could she ever hope to compete with that? "I see," she murmured, then rubbed her palms against her apron. As she looked down at it, the splashes of food, the drips and drops, the spot where she'd wiped her palms ... she expected the former Mrs. Townson didn't even own an apron, let alone dirtied it up cooking breakfast in the kitchen like some charwoman.

He followed her to the kitchen counter, but didn't sit. "What about you? Do you believe me?"

She lifted her chin, her back stiff as, like a bad penny, all Roxanne's diatribes against men came rolling over her—that men will say anything to "get what they want" and then lie about it later. "I don't know you well enough to say."

He stared at her, saying nothing at first. Then, shoulders back, head erect, he stated, "I'm not hungry." He turned and went out to the back porch.

Fighting back tears, she threw the Eggs Benedict in the garbage. She wasn't hungry either.

Around four o'clock, Carly heard a car on the driveway, followed by Hitch's barking. She went downstairs and looked out the window by the front door. She was shocked to see her older half-sister, Julia, getting out of an ancient-looking Jeep Wrangler. Carly's day had just gone from bad to horrendous.

Carly also noticed that Alex's car wasn't in the driveway. She guessed she must have fallen asleep over her books and hadn't heard him leave ... hopefully permanently taking the emaciated Skye with him.

Carly went out the front door just as Julia opened up the back of the Jeep. "Jules! What a surprise! But why are you here?"

Julia was a small woman, much shorter and thinner than Carly, but everything else about her screamed strength, power, and taking no prisoners. Her pale, ash blond hair was pulled back, twisted around and held in place with what appeared to be a wooden skewer. She wore an oversized dark green jacket that looked like it came from an Army-Navy surplus store, jeans, and brown hiking boots.

Julia glanced at Carly with dismay. "Guilt, if you must know. And I don't like it either."

Carly didn't understand. "What do you mean? Guilt? Why?"

Julia yanked hard to pull her duffel bag out from under the piles of miscellaneous junk that filled the back of her Jeep. "As I thought about it, I had to admit I should have told you I was renting out the cabin. Although you always seemed far too busy with your own business to care about me or what I'm up to. So I handled it myself. But it's your home as well, and so you shouldn't come up here expecting to be on vacation and end up having to cook and clean for some stranger." She lifted the strap of the duffel bag onto her shoulder and started up the walk to the cabin. "So I'll do it."

Carly was horrified. The one time she tasted Julia's cooking, it was tasteless goop.

Still, she was amazed that Julia had shown up to help her. Carly never forgot the time she heard Roxanne describing her three girls. "Carly is like the Papa bear—she's tall and strong, a take-charge Type A person, all practical, logical, and mind over matter. Then there's Julia who's a Mama bear—not that she's motherly, but she always looks out for underdogs, ready to fight to the finish for them. She's just a tiny thing, but so fiery and scrappy no one wants to tangle with her. Finally, there's my youngest, my beautiful Mallory. She's perfect in every way and is going to make some very rich man a beautiful trophy wife to show off to the world."

She guessed Roxanne was right about Julia's desire to help.

"Actually, the lodger has expressed to me that he sees my cooking as a benefit," Carly pointed out, hurrying to keep up with Julia's fast stride. "And I stay out of his way when he wants to work."

Julia dropped the duffel bag at the foot of the stairs. "Still, it detracts from the whole reason you've come here. Plus,"—she jutted out her chin—"since I was recently laid off, I really didn't have anything to keep me in Bend. So here I am."

"Laid off? Oh, Jules! I'm so sorry."

They walked into the great room. "Say, this place does look nice, doesn't it?" Julia, hands on hips, admired the job she'd done on the cabin. "Anyway, maybe running a B&B will become my main source of income. Who knows? At least, this way, I'll see how I like it. You two will be my first B&B customers."

"Actually, there are three of us here now."

"Three? You mean you found us another customer?" Julia actually sounded happy—a remarkable thing for her.

"No. Afraid not. Alex's girlfriend is here with us. She showed up last night."

Julia's eyebrows rose. "Is she using a separate room?"

"Yes, to my surprise," Carly said. "Although, if she has her way, it won't be for long."

"No matter how long she's here," Julia said as she went to the kitchen, "she can jolly well pay for her room."

Carly cringed at the thought. "I wouldn't."

"We aren't running a charity here. Leave it to me," Julia said as she grabbed a bottle of cold water from the refrigerator and took a long swallow. "Well, at least that means one of my worries can be set aside."

"What worry was that?"

"That the man might try to take advantage of my sister here all alone with him. And you know the story of this cabin." She held her hands up, wriggled her fingers, and made her voice low and creepy. "How the ghosts want to help others find true love, just as they had. But if the lovers reject what the ghosts offer, they'll be forever lonely and sad. *Mu-wah-ha-ha-ha.*"

"Knock it off, Jules." Carly grimaced. "That's complete nonsense and you know it. Look at our mother. She came back here year after year, and she never found true love."

"If you ask me," Julia said, her voice back to normal, "Roxanne was such a lost cause not even the cabin could help her. Or, as I've always suspected, there's no such thing as love."

"Surely, you don't believe that," Carly said.

"Of course I do. It's all lust, pure and simple."

"You can't mean that!" Carly insisted.

"Look at me." Julia shrugged. "What has the cabin done for my love life? Not that I would ever want it to. The men I meet tend to be worthless creatures."

"Don't tell that to Mallory," Carly said. Their youngest sister had a long string of boyfriends—and fiancés. But despite all of them, she'd still never made it to the altar. Almost had. And more than once. But so far "I do," played no role in Mallory's vocabulary.

Julia harrumphed. "What about you? You don't seem to be head-over-heels with anyone."

"Well, I've got Billy," Carly said.

"Yeah, right. You've mentioned him to me, what, twice? Must be a real wowzer, that one," Julia said with a sneer as she took off her jacket.

Carly couldn't help but reflect on the fact that the whole time she'd been here, she hadn't thought once about Billy. And, even more to the point, he never called, texted, or emailed her either.

She met Billy because he repaired her appliances whenever something broke, and lots of things broke down in her commercial kitchen. They would chat as he did the repairs and eventually became friends. She liked his company, but what she felt for him wasn't love, and definitely not lust. Not even close. Mainly, they contacted each other when they needed a "plus one." And their goodbyes consisted of hugs, not kisses.

It was silly of her to make up a story about him for Julia. "You're right. Billy and I will never be anything more than friends. And frankly, I wouldn't want us to be."

"Sounds right to me." Julia pulled off her boots and sprawled out on the sofa.

But then Carly's thoughts turned to last night with Alex before Skye interrupted them. If the cabin's ghosts had caused him to try to "take advantage" of her as Julia had feared, she wouldn't have minded in the least.

Carly was in the kitchen making a cheesy chicken casserole for dinner, and Julia had gone into town to buy some of her favorite wine, when Alex and Skye returned to the cabin.

Alex didn't look at all happy and, without even a hello, marched over to his computer, opened it, put on the glasses he only wore when using his computer, and proceeded to stare hard at the screen. Skye plopped herself onto the sofa, a stack of magazines in her arms.

"I'm sorry to bother you," Carly said stiffly to Alex. "But while you were out, one of my sisters turned up. Julia, the one who rented the cabin to you."

Alex leaned back in his chair, removed his glasses, and smacked the pencil he'd been holding onto the tabletop. "Your sister? Isn't that ducky! And now I suppose she's staying here, too."

Carly's jaw tightened. "She said she'll sleep out in her Jeep since all the beds are taken. She often goes camping and sleeps in it, so she doesn't mind."

"But she'll come in here at other times!" Alex stood. The look he gave her was cold and arch, as if he was doing all he could to control his temper. "I'll admit that you're quiet and your cooking more than makes up for your presence, but a gaggle of women is not what I signed up for."

"Believe me, Julia does not gaggle," Carly stated hotly. "And I doubt she'll be here long. Of course, I don't know about *your* friend." She glanced over at Skye, who hadn't bothered to look up from her magazine.

He put his glasses back on, his lips a thin, firm line. "Correction. *Your* guest. I told her to leave and offered to drive her to a hotel. *You're* the one who gave her a room."

"Not that she's paid for it," Carly said.

"Not my problem, Ms. B&B Hostess," Alex snapped.

Carly marched into the kitchen and although casting furious glances at Alex who had sat back at his computer, did attempt to keep her chopping and preparation of the evening's dinner as quiet as possible.

It wasn't long before Julia appeared at the entrance to the

great room. But the tension in the room could be cut with a knife, and even Julia backed away.

"Don't go, Jules. Come in and meet everyone," Carly said, loud enough to get Alex and Skye's attention. "This is my sister, Julia Perrin. Julia, this is Skye Kleburg, and that's Alex Townson."

Alex immediately stood. Julia gave a nod to Skye, but crossed the room to Alex, her hand outstretched to shake his. "How nice to meet you in person. I feel as if I already know you after so many emails. I hope the cabin is everything you expected."

"The cabin is quite nice," he said, his gaze darting from Julia to Carly. His expression wasn't able to hide his surprise at Julia's petite build, long nearly white blonde hair, and the bulky, over-sized man's clothing she wore. "I like it very much."

Carly understood Alex's confusion that she and Julia were sisters—it wasn't the first time she'd seen that reaction.

"Good," Julia said. "Glad to hear it."

"Of course, I was expecting to have complete privacy here. But I'll admit, Carly being here and her wonderful breakfasts made it even better than I ever expected."

Carly was stunned by Alex's praise.

Julia's eyebrows rose. "Glad to hear it. And don't worry. Carly and I know how to be quiet."

Skye suddenly got up and walked over to stand beside Alex. "You think? I don't see how he can work with all that banging and crashing in the kitchen."

Carly's knife, over the onion she was chopping, froze in mid-air.

"It's all right, Skye," Alex said. "Carly's cooking is well worth a little noise."

"Thank you, Alex. And there'll be enough chicken casserole here for anyone who wants it," Carly said.

"Chicken?" Skye spat out the word. "I don't eat chicken!"

Julia marched toward her. "Not a problem, since this is a bed and *breakfast.* We charge one-hundred-thirty a night. A credit card will be fine, and we won't run anything on it until your stay is over."

Skye's mouth dropped open. She first faced Alex who shrugged, then back to Julia who stood with her hand outstretched, palm up. "Fine." Skye had her handbag with her, found her credit card and smacked it into Julia's hand, then faced Alex. "I hope you have the decency to at least take me somewhere I can eat dinner since I'm clearly not wanted here."

"Skye, why don't you just go back to Boston?" he said wearily.

"I'm too hungry to go anywhere! And I couldn't take another of her dreadful smoothies. Let's go now."

"Yes," Carly said, arms folded as she glared at him. "Heaven forbid I inflict your friend with another of my concoctions. I think you should both leave."

Alex stared at Carly, his face filled with fury and something else—regret? Disbelief? She wasn't sure. "Why not?" he said through gritted teeth. "It's not as if I'm getting anywhere with my writing." He grabbed his jacket and stormed out the door, Skye practically running after him.

"That went well, didn't it?" Julia said, hands on hips. "But we got two night's rent out of her. To me, that's a win."

CHAPTER 18

As Carly entered the great room the next morning, she saw Julia in the kitchen area, eggs, flour, and fruit filling the counter before her. Their prior evening had been interesting as, after dinner, Carly brought out the tablecloth she'd found and Lucas Donnelly's letter. Julia was fascinated by both. She knew more details of the family's history than Carly simply because she was older, but Lucas's letter made the people involved seem more real than they ever had before.

Also, Carly was amazed to learn that Julia knew how to crochet. She was going to get some fine thread and suitable crochet hooks and attempt to mend the tears in the crochet pattern next time she came to the cabin.

But now, Julia seemed to be attempting to cook. Judging from the amount of flour on Julia, things weren't going well. "Whatever are you up to?" Carly asked.

"Busted!" Julia said. "I didn't think you'd be up this early. I remember you saying that, when you cater, it makes sense to ready as much of a meal as possible before the time came to cook. So I thought I'd help you out with breakfast by mixing the pancake batter, scrambling the eggs, and cutting up the fruit. That should make it easier when your guests come down for breakfast. Everything will be ready to go except the sausage, which requires no prep time—just a thorough cooking."

"Julia, thank you for coming here to help. It was very thoughtful. But I don't need you here cooking. I'm a pro, as you know, so it's easy for me. Please feel free to go back to Oregon. I can handle this."

Julia folded her arms and studied her sister. "I thought you'd say that, especially after Townson's little speech about how you and he were fine until me and that stick-pole woman showed up. I know when I'm not wanted."

"I didn't mean—"

"Don't worry. I'll have a nice breakfast before I start my drive home. I'm glad I came. Saw you. Saw the cabin. Lucas Donnelly's letter. I even walked down to the river at dawn. It's beautiful in the early morning with a light mist rising over the water."

"I've been here a whole week and I haven't gone down to see that," Carly admitted. "I'm glad you reminded me."

"And I met your neighbor," Julia said.

"What neighbor? We don't have any neighbors that I've ever seen."

"He seems to be a good guy. He's another 'Lucas,' although he goes by Luke. And, although he looks like he's only in his thirties, he sounds plenty old-fashioned, which I guess goes with the territory around here. He was concerned about a 'lady'—me —being all alone out there near the water, and must have thought I might swoon from the cold or something. I assured him I can take care of myself, which he seemed to like. He had a nice smile."

Carly couldn't help but gawk at Julia. She'd never, ever, heard Julia say anything nice about a man before. "You said he's a neighbor. Where is his cabin?"

"Didn't ask. I guessed you knew him. It's not like you've got more neighbors than you can keep track of."

"But I don't know him. Did he say his last name?"

"Didn't say, and I didn't ask. Hikers aren't that formal, you know." Julia wrinkled her lips. "If I'd known you cared so much I would have asked for his Facebook page!"

"I'm just curious since I've never seen him," Carly explained.

"And no wonder, since you also said you haven't gone hiking," Julia sneered. "Anyway, since you're so interested, he said he lives with his parents. I suspect he's there because he looks after them. Something about him made me guess he extends that kind of watchfulness to others. Namely, me this morning. He seemed embarrassed that he thought I might need help. I actually forgave him."

"Well now, the way you talk about him, I need to meet this paragon of gentlemanliness," Carly said with a lift of an eyebrow.

"Don't you go getting any ideas." Julia wrinkled her lips. "You know I have no interest in getting involved with any man, gentleman or not! I've watched too many women's lives fall apart because of them, starting with Roxanne's. Thanks, but no thanks."

Carly remembered that Julia never, ever, referred to their mother as anything but "Roxanne."

"You know you can't only blame the men involved," Carly said. "I think most of our mother's relationship problems were of her own doing. My father was a great guy."

"Mine wasn't," Julia said. "Not when he took off for Australia in my senior year in high school. You'd have thought he'd at least have stuck around to watch me graduate."

"He asked you to go with him, didn't he?"

"Yeah. Like how many seventeen-year-olds would want to do that? Besides, I was just a couple of months from turning eighteen, so it wasn't as if he was responsible for me any longer.

He gave the landlord back the keys to our apartment, gave me a 'graduation present' of five hundred bucks, and split. Sounds like real Father of the Year material, right?"

"I didn't realize that. I always thought your life was fine with him," Carly said. And then, since for the first time she could remember, she and Jules were being open with each other, she added, "besides, I always thought you hated me."

That seemed to give Julia pause. "Well, I did hate you when I was little." A couple of beats went by before she added, "Remember, I was only four when Roxanne walked out on me and my slime of a father. Next thing I knew, not only didn't I get to see her for over a year, but then, when she invited me to spend time with her here at the cabin that next summer, she showed up with a new husband and a new baby. You. She seemed to ooh and aah over you the way I never remembered her acting about me. That was when I decided I hated you both."

"I get it," Carly said, hating the memories this conversation stirred up. "I had similar feelings after she divorced my father and I later saw her with Mallory. In fact, I was always sure Mallory was her favorite."

"Yeah, but in a way, it could be that Mallory had it the roughest," Julia added, much to Carly's surprise.

"Mallory, the perfect?" Carly said, tongue-in-cheek.

"I know, right?" Julia said. "But after a couple of years, her father dumped her back with Roxanne and then took off for parts unknown. Mallory spent the most time living with Roxanne, and if you ask me, she's the most screwed up of the three of us because of it."

"It's funny, but you may be right," Carly said. "I never thought of her that way."

Julia shook her head. "She's the one who keeps trying to find the perfect husband—just like Roxanne did. Roxanne drummed it into her head, if you ask me. At least Mallory has the sense to walk away before she marries the wrong guy."

"Including one she left standing at the altar," Carly said, remembering how she went to New York City to attend her baby sister's wedding to some rich guy. "Everyone, it seemed, was there—except the bride. Talk about a fiasco!"

Julia laughed out loud. "Sorry I missed it. Not! All I know is, I'm fine on my own, thank you very much!"

"I'm sorry, Julia, but you shouldn't let your parents prevent you from finding someone to share your life with. Haven't you ever thought about having kids?"

Julia looked stricken. "In a word, no. Why would I when my only experience was with Roxanne harping on how I couldn't touch you or Mallory when you were babies? 'Be nice to the baby,' or 'Be quiet around the baby,' or 'Act more grown-up. I have a baby to take care of now.' It seemed the only time Roxanne ever spoke to me was to criticize."

"I remember her talking to me that way too. At least I only had one baby sister to contend with."

"Be thankful," Julia said.

Carly nodded, understanding for the first time many of the reasons Julia was the way she was. And she felt sorry for her—although she also realized much of the baggage Julia carried, she carried as well. Only not quite as heavy a load.

After breakfast, as Julia pulled her things together, Carly couldn't shake thoughts of the mysterious Lucas, or Luke, that Julia had talked about. "What does our neighbor, Luke, look like? If I see him around here, I'll say hello."

"He's got dark brown hair, fairly thick and roughly cut—almost as if he might cut it himself, although I can't imagine any man doing that these days. He's close to six feet, fairly trim, blue eyes. No, wait. I think they're gray, actually. He had a nasty cough and said it was because of the war. I guess he was in the Middle East somewhere. I didn't pursue it."

Carly blanched. Something seemed eerily familiar about this "Luke," although she wasn't sure what it was or why Julia mentioning him should bother her. "Anything else you particularly noticed?"

Julia gave Carly a sidelong glance. "Why do you care so much? I thought you're interested in Alex?"

"Wrong!"

Julia's eyebrows rose so high at that, Carly thought they might jump off her face. "All right, then, if you must know, one very interesting thing was that as we talked, Luke's gray eyes seemed to turn darker—almost a purple color, which I know is impossible."

"Yes, impossible," Carly murmured. But not nearly as impossible as her thoughts at this moment. The portrait of Elijah Donnelly seemed to change eye color at times—from gray to purple. But this Luke was a neighbor, a very human neighbor, who just happened to share a common name with an early resident of the cabin. There must be a million Lucases in this country! In fact, the only truly remarkable thing about him was that Julia seemed to find him attractive whether she would admit it or not.

"Anyway," Julia announced, "any man in his thirties who's still living with his parents must have some deep issues."

"Or, his parents are elderly, live out here in the middle of nowhere, and he's being a good son by taking care of them."

"There is that," Julia admitted. "Anyway, I'm out of here. It'll be pretty late by the time I reach home."

"You know, you really don't have to leave," Carly said. "You own the cabin too, and you aren't stopping me from working on my catering business or keeping Alex from his book."

"It's okay. I see that I'm not needed. And if somehow you can get rid of Skye, I can't help but suspect you wouldn't mind a little more alone-time with Mr. Alex Townson. Besides, I need to go back and start looking for a new graphic designs job. I'll get one—I've got the experience and the knowhow. It's just that the whole job search thing gets old really fast. If nothing else, at least I can find some online gigs to keep me in ramen and cereal —just like my college days. Anyway, I'm glad we got a chance to talk. And next time you want to use the cabin, call me. I'll make sure it's empty."

Carly decided to ignore Julia's comment about her wanting to be alone with Alex. "Have you gotten any more YourB&B reservations?"

"Not yet. I guess this place is too out-of-the-way for most people."

"That's probably true. And there isn't exactly lots to do around here."

"Whatever," Julia said, then shrugged. "Luckily, Alex's month-long rental will more than cover this year's property taxes and most of the gardening and upkeep. I think we'll be okay. So I'm out of here. I made a couple of sandwiches to take with me."

She took the sandwiches from the refrigerator and put them in a bag. Carly added two bottles of water. "I appreciate you coming all this way to help me," Carly said.

Julia frowned as she studied her a moment. "Yeah. It wasn't a bad trip. I'm surprised. Your company wasn't terrible."

"Gee, thanks," Carly said with a grin. "Yours either."

Julia snorted as she picked up her bag. She was at the front door when Carly stopped her and gave her a hug.

Julia looked stunned, then slowly let a slight smile touch her lips. Finally, she nodded and headed to her Jeep.

Carly stood at the door and watched as Julia got in the Jeep and backed out of the driveway. She was about to turn away when something odd happened.

On the side of the road just past the driveway, stood a man holding a small bouquet of wildflowers. He was dressed in brown slacks and a baggy white shirt and wearing, of all things, suspenders. He looked like an old-fashioned farmer, and Carly couldn't help but watch.

Julia stopped the car and got out as he handed her the flowers.

She held them with both hands as she lifted them toward her nose a moment. Then she bent her head forward slightly in a nod or a bow. The farmer did the same back to her. They both straightened and seemed to look at each other a long moment. And then, Julia got back into her car and slowly drove away.

Carly couldn't tell if they'd talked. They certainly hadn't touched. Yet, the air seemed to crackle all around them so forcibly, Carly could feel it all the way up at the cabin.

Just then, she heard Hitchcock galumphing down the stairs, Alex right behind him.

She put his breakfast on the counter. "My sister has gone back home," she said, keeping her expression as emotionless as possible.

"I hope I didn't drive her away," he said softly as he wrapped his long fingers around the warm coffee cup the way he did most mornings. The fact that she remembered, and enjoyed watching, such an insignificant thing about him hit her like a thunderbolt.

"No one drives Julia anywhere she doesn't want to go." With that, Carly walked out of the room, head held high and not looking back, much as she wanted to.

CHAPTER 19

"Oh my God!" Skye's shriek echoed throughout the house.

Carly rushed down the hallway to the bathroom door where the cry came from. "Skye? Are you all right?"

Skye pulled open the door. She was wearing a bathrobe, no shoes or slippers, and her hair was wet. But even wet, it no longer looked blond and straight. It had crinkled, and its color was bright green. Carly's jaw dropped. "What did you do?"

"What did *I* do?" Skye screeched. "I did nothing but wash my hair in the shower! Your shower! I was about to use my hair dryer, so I looked in the mirror and saw this! What did you do to me?"

"Nothing! I've never seen anything like that before." Carly tried to sound assuring. "I don't understand."

Alex bounded up the stairs at the sound of the cries. He gaped, speechless, at Skye.

"Look at me!" Skye cried. "What kind of place is this?"

"Calm down," Alex said. "I've heard that old pipes sometimes have copper and other minerals in them, and hair that's bleached or is full of chemicals can react to them. They turn the hair odd colors. Often,"—he tried hard not to grin—"chartreuse. Just like yours."

"Char*treuse?* You think you're funny?" She raised both hands high and pointed at her head. "This is green! Pure, ugly green. How do I get rid of it?"

"Let me try Google. I'm sure I'll find some remedies." He headed back downstairs.

Skye marched into her bedroom. "Let me know when you figure it out." She slammed the door shut.

Carly stood in the hallway a moment before deciding the best thing to do was to leave the cabin. She was sure Skye wouldn't want the breakfast she'd served Alex, and if she wanted a smoothie, she could buy one in town.

Her handbag with her car keys was in the kitchen. She didn't want to disturb Alex, who looked like he was busy searching for a solution to Skye's hair situation, so she picked up her bag and did her best to quietly leave.

But as she passed by Elijah's picture, something made her glance up at it. His carnation was the same green shade as Skye's hair.

And then he winked at her!

She must have imagined it. But still, as she hurried to the door, she was grinning broadly.

***

It was night before Carly returned. She had gone to dinner and a movie in Boise and then drove back to Garden Valley.

She didn't see Alex when she entered the great room. He must have gone out again with Skye, she thought, guessing Skye had decided not to hold him responsible for her hair problems.

She made herself a cup of coffee and took it out to the deck to help her unwind after the long drive. It wasn't difficult at all in daylight, but at night the roads were dark, and night was when lots of forest creatures came out to hunt. She wouldn't want to hurt any of them, so she drove with extreme caution.

Hitchcock stood up to greet her as she opened the French door. "Hitch, what are you doing out here?" she asked.

"He's keeping me company."

Alex was sitting in a chair on the far side of the porch, completely in the dark. She saw only his barest outline.

"I didn't realize anyone was home," Carly said.

"Just me and Hitch—my car's in the garage. Oh, and Skye's still here. Probably up in her room, tweeting and Facebooking about her horrible experiences."

"Her hair?"

"Plus, she tried to make herself a spinach, avocado, and banana smoothie, and the top of the blender flew off. Her face matched her hair color. It did nothing for her mood. I eventually found something that said lemon juice, ketchup, or apple cider vinegar should get the green out. She tried all three. Nothing worked. I think it was because she'd used a hairdryer and may have baked the color in. Then, she was cursing and carrying on so much, I tried to order her to leave. But she said she wasn't about to show up in an airport with green hair. I offered to pay for a wig, and that's when she threw a plate at me. You can add it to my bill."

Carly was almost, but not quite, ready to laugh at his tale of woe. She sat on the bench. "The good news is if she sues, she won't get anything. As far as my sisters and I go, our cupboards are bare. The only thing she could get is the cabin, and I doubt she wants it."

"As a former lawyer, let me say, green hair isn't worth a cabin. You might have to pay for her haircut, and a little for her anguish. Not much more."

"Even that might be too much for me to afford."

"I'll do my best to convince her she doesn't want her green hair publicized." His voice held a smile. "But enough about her.

Where did you go off to while I was here having fun and games?"

She told him a bit about dinner and the movie. "Actually, considering how dumb the movie was, I think I'd rather have just come back here early."

"Who could blame you?" he murmured. "It's beautiful here. I can see more stars than I ever saw back in Boston."

She smiled. "I'm glad you noticed. That's what's important."

"I'm glad there's something I do that's important," he murmured.

"Of course there is." She tried to understand why he was always so ready to put himself down. "You're important, and so is what you do."

"Sure—when I'm not ruining people's lives. Now, I write tall stories about a person I could never, in my wildest dreams, live up to."

"Hey, it's called fiction for a reason," she said with a smile, thinking it best not to ask him about ruining people's lives, much as she wondered what he meant by that. Could he have been talking about his ex-wife? Did he feel he ruined her life? She didn't want to go there. "And your readers love Rip Tarrington. I suspect they love all your ongoing cast of characters, too."

"Oh?"

She realized what she'd just said and quickly backpedaled. She was tempted to admit that she read—and loved—his books, but that would only build another bond between them, and right now, that was the last thing she wanted. Or needed. "I've read reviews of your books online. You've given enjoyment to a lot of people, and they look forward to the next one. You should feel good about yourself."

He didn't respond for a while. "It also puts more pressure on me to make the next one even better. What if I disappoint them with this new Rip-in-love story?"

For some reason, she didn't think that was the real thing

bothering him, but if he needed a diversion, she'd go along. "You'll definitely disappoint them if you don't try. As I see it, you can look at your books like a parent with several children. Each has their own personality. You'll get it to work."

He gave a heavy sigh. "This latest book will be the runt of the litter. And I'm tempted to put it in a gunny sack and drop it down the nearest well."

"You don't really mean that." She bent forward. "Besides, you haven't given the story a chance. It looks like it's still nothing but a stack of cards."

"Ever to remain so."

He sounded so unhappy, she couldn't stop herself from moving to the end of the bench near his chair and taking his hand. "Alex, listen to me. You'll get through this. You're a fine writer. Just a few days ago you sounded enthusiastic about the story."

"I know," he whispered. "What was I thinking?"

"You were thinking that you could do this," she said, and then more quietly asked, "What changed?"

His fingers tightened on hers, and then he let her go and leaned back in his chair. "Reality stepped in."

"What do you mean?" she whispered.

"The more I think about writing about love, memories of my experience come back to me." He then rose, walked to the porch railing, and faced the yard, his back to her. "On top of that, as you know, last weekend was my ex-wife's wedding day. I suspect that was the real reason I was so motivated to get out of Boston. But pictures and emails followed me here. Nothing like people trying to be 'nice' and keeping me up-to-date on all that's happening. Thanks, but no thanks."

So he did still love his wife, Carly thought. Skye had been right. She chose to remain seated and kept her voice firm as possible as she asked, "Had you two been together long?"

"Yes." He paused.

"What happened?" she asked.

He hesitated. Clearly, it was still difficult for him to talk about it. "I can't imagine that you want to hear my long tale of woe."

"Only because it's bothering you," she said. "And often, it helps to talk."

After a long silence, he said, "I've never talked to anyone about it."

"All the more reason for you to try," she said.

He nodded. "For it to make sense, you need to know I was a troublesome kid, a lousy student." She said nothing as he turned in her direction and leaned back against the rail. "My buddy suggested we join the Army. We did. My friend left after four years, but, as I've told you, I set my sights on Military Intelligence and did everything I could to get into that branch. Finally, I made it."

He paused there, and Carly suspected he was steeling himself to talk about his wife. She silently waited for him to continue.

"A couple years later, I met Francine. She was wealthy, smart, and had just gotten into law school at NYU. She seemed to find it fascinating to be going out with someone who knew all kinds of 'secrets' that I couldn't tell her. I was traveling quite a bit through Europe, Africa, and the Middle East. After a while, she got tired of a 'part-time boyfriend,' as she called me, and wanted us to be together. And I learned, she wasn't having the best time telling her fellow students that her boyfriend was in the military."

Carly smiled. "I suspect a lot of young students aren't exactly pro-military."

He nodded. "Anyway, she convinced me that I had the brains to get out of the Army and become a lawyer, too."

Uh oh, Carly thought, but said, "Nice."

"Not really. But I was smitten. I probably would have done

something illegal if she asked me to. Luckily, she never did. Anyway, we moved in together while I was in law school. She soon passed the bar and got a job at an excellent firm. Early on, I had doubts about law as a career. It didn't compare to the intrigue of Army Intelligence, but Francine convinced me to stick with it. When I passed the bar, we got married."

Carly wracked her brain for something to say. "It sounds like a good, practical plan."

"I guess. And I'm lucky to have a great role model for marriage. My parents have been happily married for over forty years. They still work together in my father's furniture store in a small town in Ohio. I imagined Frannie and I living much the same way, maybe getting law offices together, Townson and Townson. But once I actually started to practice law, it was, well, dull.

"And that's probably why I screwed up the biggest case the firm gave me. Ironically, it also made my career."

His words were confusing. "Are you saying you lost the case?"

"No. I won. And that was the problem. It was one of the firm's biggest clients—a real estate development company. They wanted to buy an entire city block in downtown Boston, tear down everything there, and put up a massive new project of high-end condos plus exclusive shops and restaurants. Of course, the current people didn't want to move. I was the junior attorney on the case.

"I managed to find precedents to absolutely crush the opposition. And did. The firm's partners were thrilled at my work and the developers got the property."

"It all sounds good," Carly said.

"It was until I got a phone call from a guy I once told you about—my mentor and friend."

Her eyebrows rose. This didn't sound good.

He heaved a sigh. "He asked how in the world I'd let it

happen? How could anyone who'd once been in intelligence not have investigated further? How could anyone who'd been in 'service'—and that's the bottom line for the military, to serve—have done what I did? I was shocked at his vehemence and disgust. And, I learned, he was right."

She was glad they were in darkness. From the quaver in his voice, she doubted she could bear the pain in his eyes as he told her all this. "What had you done?"

It took a while before he explained. "One of the buildings had been listed only as the 'Gilbertson Foundation.' I didn't know at the time it was the group home where my friend had lived."

"Oh, no," she whispered.

"The man who'd run the home for over forty years, struggling for most of those years to keep it going, had suffered a massive heart attack over the stress of fighting my firm to keep his life's work alive, and his worry over what would happen to the kids once the home was gone. I've since met him." Alex was on the verge of choking up as he all but whispered, "He's a very good man, but now is too frail ever to go back to work."

"I'm so sorry," Carly said. She couldn't just sit there and listen to his words. She got up and stepped to his side, also leaning back against the railing, her shoulder touching his. For just a moment, she put her arm around his shoulder and gave him a friendly hug, touching her head to his, and then let him go. It wasn't much, she knew, but she could only hope, for the moment, it was enough.

It took a long while before he said anything more, but the simple fact that he didn't move indicated he liked and accepted her support. Finally, he spoke. "If I'd done my job right, I would have found out what was in that building. Instead I took the law firm's word that it was just another office that could easily move anywhere with the money they'd get from the developer. But they didn't get nearly enough to make the modifications necessary to turn a building into a group home."

"Oh, Alex, it wasn't only your fault," she whispered. Her heart bled for him, having seen enough in just a few days to understand how devastating this had been for him.

"But it was! The legal team actually knew what was there! But I was new at all this; I was green, and it showed. I didn't check deep enough, and I have to live with that." He sounded beyond bitter, beyond distressed.

"What could you have done?" The ever-practical Carly asked, even while wishing she could find words to ease his burden. She stopped leaning against the rail at that, but stood up straight and faced him. There was just enough starlight to meet his eyes.

"I could have fought it. Gotten the developer to pay the group home more money to give it some hope of being able to reopen somewhere else. Tried to make some accommodation for them. Instead, I lost a friend, nearly killed a good man, and had a bunch of kids who needed the structure of a group home sent to foster care where who knows what happened to them."

"Is that why you left law?"

"It was the last straw. No one cared what we'd done. My own wife couldn't understand why I was so bothered. She had a fit when I gave the bonus money from my firm for my 'good work' to the Gilbertson House, to help them salvage what they could."

Carly had no words.

"I turned to writing thrillers to help the place out, but oddly, the better my books did, the angrier Francine became. I got to know the people running the home, and some of the kids there. They're good people working in a tough situation, and I was happy to donate big chunks of my advances to them. Anyway, when book four came out, Francine filed for divorce."

"So she never understood …?" Carly asked, wondering how Alex's wife couldn't see what that lawsuit had done to him.

"Never. And going through the divorce …" He stopped and once again turned away from her, facing the orchard. All she could see in the dark was the bend of his head, and the rigid form of his arms as his hands tightly gripped the porch railing. She could also hear the tension and pain in his voice, and through them, all but feel the crushing loneliness and waves of disappointment he must have felt. "All I can say is, when we divorced, I learned love can have an expiration date."

Carly remembered hearing a similar lament from Roxanne. Her mother's words haunted her to this day, and to hear Alex speak them as well was soul-shattering. She had hoped that perhaps true, undying love could be a reality, but now she had confirmed—by a person she cared about—that it couldn't. "For some people," she whispered, "words like 'for richer, for poorer, in sickness and in health' are noise without meaning."

"So it seems," he said. "And now, my publisher expects my next book to be about finding true love. What a joke! And then I learned that Francine was going to get married again."

"That must have been hard," Carly said.

"It surprised me how much it hurt."

"Well, I'm sure you have plenty of women lined up to take her place," she said with a small smile.

Alex turned towards her once more. "You wouldn't think that if you ever talked to Francine about me."

"Who cares what she has to say?" Carly stated vehemently. She placed her hand on his upper arm. "It's clear she never understood or appreciated you. If she did, she'd never have talked you into leaving a career you loved for one she enjoyed, and she certainly wouldn't have discouraged your writing!"

His gaze met hers. Even in the dark, she could see how much he appreciated her words. He took both her hands in his. "Thank you. You're a good person, Carly."

"But it's true. And all of it happened in the past," she said, trying her best to encourage him as their fingers intertwined. "It's over."

"Except for the kids," he said softly letting her go. "They gave me a big advance on this latest book, hoping to push it to the *New York Times* list. If I can only get it written, get the advance released upon receipt of an 'acceptable' manuscript, it'll finally make the Gilbertson House solvent in its new location."

"You'll do it," she said. "Because you're a fine man, Alex Townson. A caring man. Whether you know it or not."

"Only you would say that." He let his hands slide along her arms, from her shoulders to her hands as the heat rose between them, a desire, raw, yet sweet. Her gaze dropped to his mouth. He took hold of her waist, drawing her closer. His nearness made her heart beat even faster. But then she remembered that she was leaving soon. That his ex-girlfriend was still in the cabin. And that he hardly needed more complications in his life.

She put her hands on his shoulders. "It's time for me to go inside," she murmured and took a step back.

He dropped his hands and nodded as if he understood how difficult the situation was for her. She asked herself if she was being foolish. He wanted to kiss her, and would have. And she wanted him to. What was the harm?

Neither moved.

But then, she placed her hand against the side of his face, a loving gesture although a poor substitute for a kiss. She hoped he understood. Only then did she find the strength to walk away.

CHAPTER 20

Alex had been surprised to find a note from Carly at breakfast saying his food was in the warming drawer and coffee was in a carafe. But Carly herself was nowhere to be seen.

He wondered if he had gone too far the night before, telling her about his past. Maybe after she thought about it, she'd come to the realization, as Francine had, that there was something fundamentally wrong with him that caused people to turn away or give up on him.

It wasn't until later that afternoon as he moved from the sofa to his desk, that he spotted her through the French doors standing out in the backyard cutting deadheads from the tall, thick rose bushes that grew alongside the porch railing. Her hair was pulled into a ponytail, and she wore shorts and a T-shirt. She looked amazingly cute out there.

He told himself to go back to his nonsensical story that he once again hated, and to leave her alone. But all of a sudden, he found himself out on the front porch saying, "Could you use some help?"

He almost wished he could blame such a foolish step on the

ghosts, but he knew he'd gotten out there under his own power. Besides, the ghosts seemed to be focussing their attention on Skye now. And who could blame them?

He shuddered at the realization that he was making a joke like that. Much as he firmly didn't want to believe there was such a thing as ghosts, this place was making him have his doubts. But any ghost that had the good sense to pick on Skye, who still refused to leave, was okay with him.

"It's really hot out here today," Carly said, using her arm to wipe the sweat from her brow. "But these rosebushes will look much better when they bloom again."

"How soon?"

"A week, ten days. You'll be able to enjoy them."

"But you won't," he said softly, the realization hitting like a knife to the gut.

Her smile vanished, just as his had. She wants to stay, he thought. Maybe …

He descended the steps.

"These flowers haven't been cared for in months," she averted her eyes from him to the flowers. "I'm cutting off not only the dead ones, but any stems that are too long and spindly. That helps new growth come in strong and healthy."

He picked up an extra hand trimmer from the basket of gardening tools beside her and after studying the roses before him, he chose a long rose stem with a dead flower at the end. "Now what?"

"Right there." She pointed to a nub along the stem. "Cut right above that bump."

He did as told, then went on to do the same with two more deadheads.

Carly nodded. "You've got it. I appreciate the help, by the way. My back is aching. I'm not used to bending so low." She put her hands on the small of her back and did a backwards stretch.

His mouth went dry as her posture emphasized the lush

figure he'd given far too much thought to over the past few days. He suspected she had no idea what a beautiful woman she was. "No problem." He croaked the words, turning from her to try to concentrate on the roses and not on the woman beside him. Everything about her appealed to him in a way he hadn't felt in a long time. How was he supposed to let her return to a job she hated and never see her again? "I like being out in the air," he said. "Sometimes staring at a blank computer screen gets really frustrating."

She smiled. "I can imagine. But you're a pro. You'll be fine."

"So they tell me."

The two worked in silence for a while, then Alex said, "I just want to thank you for letting me bend your ear yesterday. It did feel good to vent."

"Glad to be of service," she said. "And I really do think you're being too hard on yourself. You made a mistake, and you've done far more than most people would to make up for it. You should be proud."

"I'm not sure about that, but thank you."

Alex went back to concentrating on the flowers. Or trying to. He couldn't help but watch her work—or play, considering how happy she looked out here, as if the issues that usually weighed her down were gone. Her skin, that had been so pale when he first met her, now had a healthy tan, and her cheeks a natural blush. Her eyes sparkled more than ever, her nose seemed more pert—although even he knew such a thing wasn't possible—and her lips... How he wished he had ignored Hitchcock's barks and Skye's arrival, and everything else the other night, and had simply kissed her the way he wanted to.

Maybe then Skye would have seen them and left. Maybe...

But who knows where such kisses might have led?

And then what? She wasn't a woman to treat lightly. He knew if she fell in love, it would be completely—just like in those old-time musicals she was so fond of.

He was afraid he wasn't right for someone like her, anyway. From all he'd been told, he didn't know how to return such love. And if he couldn't love her as she deserved, to lead her on would be cruel.

And there must be someone back in San Francisco. She'd never said; but then, he'd never asked.

He pruned the roses silently for several more minutes, but then couldn't hold back any longer. "So, tell me, are you seeing anyone in San Francisco?"

She looked surprised. "Why do you ask?"

He shrugged. "Just curious."

She didn't respond, and he wondered why not. Finally, she said, "There's … someone."

His heart sank; of course there was. "You never talk about him."

She nodded and, again, a long moment passed before she said, "I suppose not."

Was something off here? She didn't sound like a woman in love. "Have you known him very long?"

"Yes." When he said nothing and waited, she added, "About seven years. But we only started dating some five or so years ago."

Did she just say … "Five years?"

"That's right."

Curiouser and curiouser. "So why haven't you two tied the knot?"

"I told you. My business is too unsettled."

"And what about his?"

"What about it? He has nothing to do with my work."

"Does he ever talk about sharing the burden of the business with you?"

"Of course not." She was growing irritated. "He's an appliance repairman. He doesn't know what to do in a kitchen. Or in a garden nursery, for that matter."

"But what about the business side of things?"

"He's got a boss. His company gives him health insurance, a 401(k) plan, unemployment insurance, and all kinds of things. In a word, he's got it much easier than I do."

Alex nodded, then, after a while asked, "And does he realize what an idealist you are?"

Her pruning shears stilled. "Me? An idealist? Where in the world did that come from? I'm the most practical person you'll ever want to meet. Everyone says so."

"It came from observation. If nothing else, as a writer, I've got to observe the world around me. And you're clearly an idealist not only about business but also about your personal life. You've settled on a business because of obligations, and I can't help but see it's eating at you. You've been with your fellow in San Francisco a long time. Have you ever considered that you might be 'settling' with him as well?"

She put down her shears and, hands on hips, glared at him. At the same time, she looked close to tears. "That's a terrible thing to say!"

"Is it?" he asked. She had so much going for her, so much potential, and she was throwing it away because she felt obligated to a business she'd inherited. And now, it also seemed she felt obligated to some dweeb who'd hung around her for five years and didn't have the sense to put a ring on her finger. Anger bubbled up in him, and he wasn't even sure why. So he focused it on her. What was wrong with the guy? And why did she put up with him? "I'm saying what I'm seeing." His tone was harsh. Too harsh.

Her face reddened and her voice grew louder with each word. "What you're seeing? *Seeing?* I don't think so!"

That red hair of hers went into overdrive. "If I haven't hit a nerve, why are you so angry?"

"Because you think you know it all! And you're condescending!"

That hurt. "Condescending? Carly, that's the last thing I am around you."

"You don't know me at all. And you have no business thinking you do!" Carly started toward the house, but then spun around and marched back to face him. Tears filled her eyes. "You called me an idealist. Well, let me tell you, idealists eventually grow up and realize that the world doesn't work to make everything sweetness and light for them. Paths aren't always strewn with flower petals. Often, there are thorns along the way. Big, ugly ones!"

"Hey, I'm sorry. I didn't mean to make you cry," he said. He took hold of her arms wanting to pull her closer and hold her until she stopped hurting.

But she shoved him away, hard, and wiped her eyes. "I'm not crying!" She spun away from him and turned toward the cabin.

"Wait!" He plucked a rose that had fully bloomed and would soon be losing its petals. "This is what you love. This is where your heart is."

He held the rose toward her.

She stared at it a long moment, then shook her head and stormed into the house.

Carly was too restless to remain alone in her room until dinnertime. She kept playing in her mind all Alex had told her about his past, how he had grappled with his wife's disillusion with the kind of man he really is, and his continued feelings of guilt for the way his research had caused a group home to be shut down. He had opened up to her, and after all that, how did she help him deal with it? She lied about her relationship with Billy in San Francisco and then got mad at him for calling her an "idealist." What was wrong with her? It was as if she was more concerned with protecting her own heart than offering compassion to a man who had clearly reached out to her for help.

Carly decided to walk down by the river. Maybe there she could stop thinking about Alex and focus instead on the beauty of nature around her. She changed into jeans and rugged soled shoes.

She headed downstairs and as she walked to the door, Hitchcock waddled over to her as quickly as his girth allowed. He pushed his nose against his leash and looked up at her with melt-your-heart soulful eyes. "Okay, boy. I get it."

Much as she hated to face Alex again after the way she'd acted, she couldn't ignore the dog's pleading. She went into the great room. Alex was sitting at the table staring at his computer, and Skye was propped up on the sofa studying fashion in one of her ever-present magazines. Her hair was pulled up into a green knot. When she gazed at Carly, the venom in her eyes was jaw-dropping. Carly looked away immediately.

"Alex, I'm going down to the river," Carly said in as cold a voice as she could manage. "Hitchcock wants to go for a walk. Do you mind if I take him?"

Alex said nothing, but simply stared at her, his expression unreadable. He then stood and stretched his arms and shoulders. "Actually, that sounds like a great idea. I think I'll join you. I've been sitting far too long."

"No need," Carly said, backing away.

Alex headed toward the door, as if he hadn't even heard her saying she didn't want or need his company.

"Good idea." Skye swung her long legs off the sofa and stood. "I'd love to get out of this cabin."

Carly looked at Skye's short shorts and thin-soled sandals with heels.

"You might want to change shoes," Carly said to her. "To get to the river you have to walk down a path that's somewhat steep, and the brush gets fairly thick."

Skye gave Carly's jeans and shoes a sniff and said, "I'll be fine."

"But those sandals—"

"They're Jimmy Choo's," Skye announced as if that explained everything.

Carly said no more but, ever the "caterer," went to the refrigerator, grabbed three beers and a bottle opener, put them in a tote and followed Skye out the door.

In no time Carly understood why Skye wasn't worried about the pathway. As soon as the trail became the slightest bit difficult, she grabbed Alex's arm and insisted he help her.

Soon, Carly and Hitchcock were far ahead of the other two, since Skye's sandals wobbled unsteadily with almost every step. More than once, Skye stopped so she could tighten or loosen the straps.

On the opposite bank, among the trees, Carly spotted a group of elk grazing. Elk thrived in this area not only because of the river but also due to the area's plentiful vegetation, cabins, and enough human activity to keep most of their natural predators and hunters away.

Carly sat on a felled tree trunk and waited for the other two to catch up. Hitchcock stepped into the water far enough to wet his feet, but listened when Carly stopped him from going in too far. The river bank was steep, and in only a few feet, it went from wetting his paws, to deep enough to be over his head. Natural water dog that he was, Carly knew he would have loved to go for a swim. She didn't dare let him, although the thought of Skye's reaction if the big guy stood near her and shook water off his coat was enough to make Carly laugh out loud.

"What's so funny?" Alex said as he reached her.

Her heartbeat thrummed at his nearness. She really needed to get over him. "I was just ... uh ... seeing how happy Hitchcock looks out there in the water."

"He does, doesn't he," Alex said, then sat beside Carly on the log. Thoughts of the last time he was so close washed over her, making her want to reach for him, to apologize. Instead, she immediately jumped up and then backed away a few steps.

Skye immediately took her place beside Alex, folded her arms, and stared at the river. "It kind of makes me want to join him."

"I suggest you don't," Carly said with a frown.

Skye harrumphed. "It's hot and ugly here, but the river water looks cool. Come on, Alex."

With that, Skye ran to the water's edge, took off her sandals, then looked back at Alex.

Alex glanced at Carly. She had been watching him, but as soon as he faced her, she turned her head trying, unsuccessfully, to ignore him. He then called out to Skye, "Don't go in far. It gets steep fast." He pulled off his shoes and socks, rolled up his pants legs, and went to the river.

"Oh, it's so cold!" Skye cried, putting a toe in.

"The mountain snows are melting," Alex said.

"I don't like it!" Skye announced, but all of a sudden, she nose-dived, head first, into the water.

"Skye!" Alex yelled, taking careful steps toward her.

Carly ran to the water's edge.

Skye immediately stood up. The river was only up to her knees.

"Don't go any deeper," Alex ordered. "Grab my hand!"

But Skye slapped his hand away. "Who pushed me?" she shrieked as she splashed her way onto dry land. She was sopping wet.

"Pushed you?" Alex asked. "No one."

"Somebody shoved me face first into that … that ice! Who did it?" She faced Carly and glared. One of her fake eyelashes was gone.

"Don't look at me," Carly said. "I'm still dry."

At that, Hitchcock approached. He apparently had taken

their distraction as an opportunity to go swimming, and now he shook his very large, very wet body, dousing all of them with sheets of river water.

"I hate all of you!" Skye screamed as she stuck her feet in her sandals. "And if I get pneumonia, I'll sue!" She marched off in the direction of the cabin, already slipping and sliding on the relatively flat ground.

Alex went back to the log, put on his shoes and socks, and unrolled his pant legs. Instead of sitting on the log, he sat on the ground and leaned back with his head resting on it, his legs stretched out before him.

Hitchcock wandered around checking the area.

"If you want to head back to the cabin, it's fine by me," he said to Carly. "I'm going to stay here a while and I know I'm not your favorite person at the moment. I... I was talking out of turn. How you live your life is none of my business, and I apologize."

Carly couldn't help but to forgive him, especially since most of what he said was spot on. "It's okay. You did nothing wrong," she said. Part of her said she should leave him there, let him be alone. And to be alone, herself. The other part wanted nothing so much as to stay with him. "Maybe it's best to let Skye cool off."

He said nothing. She hesitated, but then sat on the ground beside him. He looked so comfortable, she emulated his position, and leaned back against the log, her arms under her head as she raised her face to the sun. "This feels good."

"It does."

She saw him shut his eyes. She told herself to remember this moment in the lonely days to come, this very special moment because being next to Alex, by the river, was exactly where she wanted to be.

After several peaceful minutes, he sat up and opened beers for them.

"Those are some pretty wildflowers." Alex pointed at a white cluster on a hill above the river.

She could scarcely believe that he had noticed the delicate white petals. "They're Idaho's state flower, the syringa. In late spring, their peak blooming season, they can turn an entire hillside snowy white. This particular species is called Lewisii, named after Meriwether Lewis, who first described them when he and William Clark crossed Idaho on the way to the Pacific."

Alex had an odd look on his face as a slight smile formed on his lips. He stared out at the river and the land beyond as he said, "You know, for most of my life, Lewis and Clark were simply two guys mentioned in history books. Now, I find myself sitting by a river like one they probably crossed a little over two hundred years ago. The land around me is still natural and probably looks like it did when they first saw it. It's all kind of amazing."

Her heart filled to hear his words. "That's true. And the syringa honors them to this day."

"It does. I'm glad," he whispered and then faced her with a nod. His reaction mirrored her own thoughts and feelings about this area, feelings she had forgotten over the years. But now, with him, they were awakened. And, as she gazed at his handsome face, and contemplated the fine, caring mind behind a magnificent facade, her emotions slipped toward what she could only regard as love. Somehow, she had to stop them ... before it was too late.

His head cocked, his gaze intense as he studied her face.

"What?" she asked.

"Your eyes... they..."

"They?"

He swallowed and then blinked several times. "Nothing. It's just the play of the light, or maybe because we were talking about something you love. It's good to see."

His words made no sense to her, but the way her heart

pounded as she listened to him, she knew that whatever he might have been referring to wasn't as much *what* they were talking about as *who* she was speaking with. She sucked in her breath, reminding herself it wasn't wise to care so much about him.

"A breeze is coming up." She picked up the empty beer bottles and caps and put them in to her tote bag to discard in the cabin's trash bin. "I guess it's time to head back."

He took her arm. "Stop. We need to talk."

She shrugged him off. "Sure. But we can talk back at the cabin. Anytime." She ran ahead of him and called Hitchcock to join her. "Come on, boy. Let's go home."

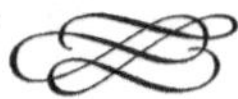

CHAPTER 21

Carly reached the cabin before Alex and Hitchcock. As she entered, she saw an older, gray-haired man sitting on the sofa. He was quite thin, wore a dark blue wool suit, and had a small suitcase at his feet. As soon as he noticed her, he stood.

Don't let it be that Jules found another boarder, she prayed. If so, where was she supposed to put him? "Can I help you?" she asked.

"Pardon me for letting myself in," the man said. "Your front door was unlocked, and it's warm outside with this suit. I expected to find Alex Townson here."

"Jack! I told you I didn't need you here," Alex bellowed as he strode into the room.

Carly spun around at Alex's voice. He sounded furious.

"Calm down, Alex." The man called "Jack" appeared flustered. "I heard Skye is here."

"Where did you hear that?" Alex demanded.

"From Skye. Where else?" Jack's voice remained calm and controlled. "Is it true?"

"She's here," Alex muttered. "In fact, I thought she'd be in the house."

"If so, she ignored me. Typical Skye," Jack said, his jaw tight. "Her being with you wasn't the plan."

"You think I invited her here?!"

"If not, why didn't you send her home?" Jack demanded.

Alex crossed the room to the refrigerator. Carly's head bobbed from one man to the other, knowing she should leave but unable to tear herself away.

Alex took two waters from the refrigerator and held one out to Jack. Both men immediately took a drink.

"Believe me, I tried," Alex said. "But she's a paying guest, which is important to the owners here. And besides, I'd have better luck talking to a door."

Carly was surprised to hear Alex had picked up on her and Julia's money problems. But then, they were probably pretty obvious.

Jack stuck out his bottom lip as if in thought, then said, "I'm afraid I know why."

"What do you mean?" Alex asked.

"Well ..." The newcomer's gaze went to Carly, who still stood by the front door.

"I'm sorry," Alex said. "I should have introduced you two. Carly, this annoying fellow is my literary agent, Jack Bellar. Jack, meet an owner of the cabin, Carly Fullerton."

"Your agent?" she said with surprise as she held her hand out to the older man. "How do you do, Mr. Bellar. If you were, by chance, hoping to stay here, I'm afraid we're booked up."

"Don't worry about me," Jack said. "I'll be just fine. I don't mind sleeping on the sofa or anywhere else. I'm here for one reason only." He turned back to Alex. "That is to do whatever I can to stop that nattering ninny from bothering my client so that he can *finish the first draft of his book!* I'm sorry I ever introduced her to him!"

"I see," Carly said, taking a step back at the agent's vehemence. "Well, I can call around and try to find you accommodations close by, if you wish."

"Let me think about it, my dear," Jack said.

"Thanks, Carly," Alex told her in a tone that indicated she should leave. Now. He turned to Jack. "You were saying about Skye?"

Carly started up the stairs and was only halfway up when Jack responded. "A few days ago Skye called and asked about you. I told her everything was fine—more than fine, as I was talking to a Hollywood agent about a possible series for the Rip Tarrington books—Netflix, Prime, or something similar."

"Oh, no," Alex raked his fingers through his hair.

"Sorry, pal," Jack said. "I was trying to help, trying to let her know you not only didn't need your ex-wife but also didn't need her. That you're fine on your own."

"Except that you were talking to Skye," Alex said with a heavy sigh.

"And I can't help but think that's what spurred her sudden desire to see the wilds of Idaho," Jack said.

Guilt struck Carly over her eavesdropping. And besides, she had heard enough. She hurried up to her bedroom.

Alex went out to buy pizza for dinner instead of simply requesting a delivery. Carly could see that he wanted—or needed—to be on his own for a while. Jack was hitting the beer hard, and Skye remained in her room sulking.

Carly made herself a cup of coffee and went out to the back porch to drink it. She wanted nothing to do with Jack or Skye, and wasn't pleased when Jack joined her, a fresh bottle of beer in hand.

He had hardly acknowledged her presence up to that point

and frankly struck her as a snob. She stiffened with suspicion as he peered at her from under thick, wiry eyebrows that were a variety of shades of gray.

Finally, he sat on the far end of the bench she was using. "I had the impression from Alex that you came here expecting to have the cabin all to yourself."

No "Hello," or "How are you?" or "Thank you for letting me stay here tonight even though you have no room for me and I didn't even offer to pay you for giving me a roof over my head." Not that she would have taken his money.

"You heard correctly," she said.

He removed the cap from his beer. "It sounded as if the two of you had worked out a compatible schedule until Skye showed up."

She didn't quite know how to answer that. It was clear Jack had no use for Skye, but it wasn't her place to trash the woman. "I like to think Alex would have been content here," she said, "had we been able to share the cabin the way we had planned. Alex said he felt as if he was calming down enough to concentrate on writing. That might have been wishful thinking, but I believed him."

Jack took a long drink from his beer bottle before commenting. "Alex isn't one for positive thinking. His problem is the opposite. He'll brood on the negative."

"So I've noticed," she admitted.

He put his bottle on the side table. "A lot is riding on this book."

"He's had several best sellers," Carly said. "Why is he under so much pressure with this one?"

Jack grimaced. "His publisher has extensive marketing plans for it. We not only need to get it in on time, but it needs to provide an additional element to Rip Tarrington's character. A deepening, so to speak. That's why I'm anxious about seeing the first draft. I want to make sure it's perfect before we send it to his editor."

"Perfect? That's a lofty standard."

He looked at her a long time, as if to decide how much he should or shouldn't tell her. "This latest contract was a big one—a huge advance. And they want the story to live up to the money provided. Right now, he's dealing—to my mind—with some strange writer's block. But he can get past it. I know he can. He needs to get over what's bothering him and write."

"And if he doesn't?" Carly asked.

Jack shrugged. "Who knows? Worst case, they cut him loose, and his name is mud in New York publishing circles. Best case, they give him an extension. But that will only happen if they're sure he can deliver."

"I see," Carly said. Before hearing this, she had no idea how the publishing industry worked, or that things could go that bad. "But this writer's block, or whatever it is, sounds as if it's because the story line his editor wants doesn't appeal to him."

"Ah! So he has talked to you about it. I'm afraid what he's saying is just an excuse. He can write whatever he needs to. There's something more going on, and I'm here to see if I can help." Jack shook his head. "I don't know what's wrong. And he's too close-mouthed and private to tell me. If I knew, I'd tell him how to fix it."

Carly also wished she could help. She suspected Alex's difficulties with the "love interest" his editor wanted had to do with his ex-wife's leaving him, and Alex's tendency to blame himself when things went wrong.

Jack took another healthy swallow of the beer. "I've noticed in the short while I've been here," he said, "that Alex listens to you."

She turned toward him in surprise. "He does?"

"I know he does. Whenever you're in the room, you're the one he most closely watches. You're the one whose approval he seems to look for. And when you weren't with us, he spoke extremely well of you and his time at the cabin with you."

Jack's words elated her. "That's nice to hear, but you may be seeing more than exists. I have the impression Alex still hasn't gotten over his ex-wife."

He grimaced. "That's not it. His ex was smart, beautiful, and knew how to get him to do what she wanted. He hates failure and sees his marriage as a failure, but that's different from pining over his ex. I'm positive he's not still in love with her. He might even be wondering why he ever was!"

The way Jack was grimacing, Carly could imagine he would have no qualms about getting rid of anyone he no longer wanted in his life.

"I can tell you one thing," Jack continued. "I've never seen Alex look at any woman the way he looks at you."

She eyed Jack sharply. Was he just saying that? She couldn't imagine…

"Tell me," Jack said. "Is there someone you're seeing? That you're serious about?"

She hesitated, then took the most cautious route. "I guess you could say there is."

Jack lifted one eyebrow and seemed about to say more when Alex's voice called out from the great room. "The pizza has arrived."

CHAPTER 22

"So you were enjoying the great outdoors, Jack," Alex said when Jack and Carly came back inside. "That's a new one."

"We were having a chat about the joys and benefits of rural life," Jack said. "All this quiet. Close to nature. Sometimes, in a bustling city, it's easy to forget about simple pleasures…Oh, my God." His mouth dropped open as he looked at Skye and her green hair, now pulled into a small lime-colored knot at the top of her head.

"I think nature here is boring," Skye said, ignoring Jack as she began opening the pizza boxes on the kitchen island. "Oh, good! You got a veggie pizza for me."

"It has gluten," Carly said, earning an ugly sneer from Skye.

As Jack stared at Skye, he began softly singing, *"Put de lime in de coconut an' drink'um bot' up."* Then he grinned. "Don't know why that old song popped into my head."

Skye looked ready to murder him.

As they ate, they talked a little about rural life, but soon switched to Boston, New York, and people there. Alex tried to include Carly in the conversation, but she quickly became lost in a blur of names.

After dinner, Skye said, "This place is too quiet. There's no TV, no radio, no internet to speak of—once in a blue moon, outside, you can get cell service. It's awful. Does anyone have music loaded onto their phone? I only use streaming, so I never bothered."

"There are some old CDs and tapes," Alex said. "In fact, you can hear Carly's mother singing on some of them."

"Her *mother?*" Skye looked simultaneously amused and horrified.

"How interesting," Jack said. "What did she sing?"

"Show tunes, mostly," Carly said. "She performed quite a few shows off-Broadway and was part of the touring troupe for some bigger musicals. But it was many years ago."

"I adore show tunes," Jack said. "I used to go to Broadway shows all the time. There were lots of shows I couldn't get enough of. *Les Miserables* was probably my absolute favorite."

"My mother also loved it, but it's too expensive for most little theater groups," Carly added. "She often performed in shows like *Oklahoma* and *Seven Brides for Seven Brothers.* A wagon and a bale of hay and you've got your set."

"Classics!" Jack exclaimed. "Where are your mother's tapes?"

Carly showed him the box and then switched on the cassette player.

"Never heard of them," Skye's tone making it clear how bored she still was.

Jack flipped through the tapes, each labeled with the songs performed. He put on one and they listened and chuckled as Roxanne sang about a "surrey with a fringe on top." Jack, and even Skye, had to admit that Roxanne had a clear, powerful voice. Most of the songs were light, jaunty, and carefree, but she surprised them when she softly sang "Where Is Love?" from

Oliver. It was so emotionally sung they all stopped talking to listen.

The song ended, and the cassette stopped as if it had reached the end of the tape.

"Absolutely beautiful," Jack murmured.

And then, to everyone's surprise, the cassette started up again with Roxanne singing "If I Loved You."

Carly couldn't help but look at Alex. He met her eyes as he, too, seemed to remember their earlier conversation about *Carousel* and the heartbreaking song about a couple too afraid to admit their love for each other.

Alex stood, and to Carly's amazement, held out his hand.

Skye gawked at them and was about to speak when Jack jumped up and pulled her to her feet. "Let's dance." He took her in his arms and danced her away from Alex.

Carly scarcely noticed them. The world seemed to stop as Alex awaited her response. Once again, she stepped into his arms. The first time they danced together had been wonderful, but tonight was much more. He held her close and let his cheek rest against her hair. She loved the way she fit into his arms, as the scent of soap and sunshine and the river that clung to his skin and hair enveloped her. Her arms tightened around him and she shut her eyes, allowing herself to become lost in the man and the music. She had once heard that dancing was an invitation to fall in love. It was, she thought, absolutely true.

Too soon, the song ended, and the cassette abruptly stopped.

Skye had ejected it. "I think that's enough dancing for tonight," she loudly declared. "Alex needs his rest so he can write tomorrow. It's too bad you showed up, Jack. Your being here wasted his entire evening. I would have expected you to realize that, but I guess you had to see for yourself that he really is trying to work here."

"The only one who's disrupting anything around here, Skye,

is you." Jack glared fiercely at her. "I suggest you be the one to leave."

Carly and Alex stood apart, the warm, intimate mood destroyed by the growing cacophony.

Skye got right in Jack's face. "You have some nerve! You come here and badger him about his book. You want him to think he needs you, but you know he doesn't. And he certainly doesn't need to give you fifteen percent of everything he earns through his own hard work."

Jack's eyes flashed with anger. "He also knows he never would have gotten such lavish contracts if it weren't for me."

Skye folded her arms. "I'll admit you were good for Alex once. But no more. I believe the best thing for him would be to break this contract. Then, he'd be done with that publishing house as well as you."

"That's madness!" Jack's voice bellowed, deep and loud. "Do you know what something like that could do to his reputation in the business? Do you realize—"

"*Stop!*" Alex shouted. "Both of you. Frankly, I don't want *either* of you here. I'm sorry, Jack, that you came all this way for nothing. But really, you've got to let me do this my own way."

"But your own way isn't working!" Jack shouted back.

"You need me here," Skye shrieked.

"Like a toothache!" Alex snapped.

"I came here to help you, Alex," Jack roared.

"Don't listen to him, sweetie." Skye assured him. "We'll handle this together! We'll get you a movie deal, and we'll handle it ourselves."

Jack faced Skye, his face beet red. "You think you're some kind of Hollywood expert now? That you know how to negotiate such a tremendous deal? I don't think so!"

"I'm an expert in one thing." Skye was all but screaming. "I know a con artist when I see one. And that's you!"

"I'm asking you both to leave." Alex looked like a balloon that had been deflated.

Skye grabbed his arm. "I'm doing all this for you!"

"Go away, Skye!"

"How can you say that?" she shrieked.

"Easy!" He jerked his arm free.

"You're hateful! I love you, but you aren't capable of love!"

"It's good you're leaving then, isn't it?"

She folded her arms and glared at him, as did Jack.

Alex's gaze jumped from one to the other. "I can't do this anymore." He strode toward the door.

"Alex, wait! You don't mean that," Jack bellowed.

Alex stopped. "Don't I? I came out here to be alone, to write, and at every step I've had roadblocks thrown in my way. If I'd been able to do what I wanted, I know things would be different. But all of you"—his eyes took in Carly as well—"decided you know better than me what I need, what I want, what I should do. Well, no more. I've had it."

He left the cabin with Hitchcock following.

Carly stared at Jack and Skye, both standing with their mouths hanging open and gawking at the door. Something told her Alex had never crossed either of them that way before.

She was proud of him. But he'd included her in his complaint. And he'd been right to. She had ignored his needs as she worked to get what she wanted without understanding the pressures he was under.

She wasn't all that much better than the two before her. She faced them. "Splendid job, guys. And me, too, now that I'm tarred with the same brush." Her hands were on her hips, her heart pounding in a mixture of fury and heartache. "I wonder if he has any idea where to go. He'll have to find a place for himself and Hitch, get settled and get used to the changes all over again. Or he might go back to Boston and give up."

"He doesn't mean it," Jack grumped.

"He's just being dramatic." Skye moved her head as if to toss her long hair, then grimaced as if remembering the green knot it had become.

"He meant it all right," Carly said. "Of course, he could have just stayed here, been left alone, and might have gotten some work done. But you two couldn't stand that, could you?"

"You think I'd leave him here alone with you?" Skye sneered. "I've seen how you look at him."

Carly's eyebrows rose. "Are you actually admitting that *you* are jealous of *me*?"

Skye's cheeks reddened. "You're right. That would be silly of me, wouldn't it?"

Jack eyed Skye. "She has a point, you know. We're both doing more harm than good here. What if he and that hairy monster he calls a dog were to go wandering around trying to find a different place to stay? Or even worse, what if he does go back to Boston?"

Skye still looked furious, but somehow Jack's words seemed to penetrate. "I don't know."

"We should leave him here," Jack continued. "Give him the quiet he's asked for. And even though you're worried about her, Carly's leaving at the end of the week. Alex will be here alone."

"She won't be here?" Skye's eyes narrowed as she glared at Carly.

"He's right," Carly said. "I return to San Francisco this weekend."

"Well, it isn't as if I'm worried about competition." Skye pouted. "I was only trying to be helpful."

Jack took one of her arms. "Maybe you're too much of a distraction. The guy's only human." She scowled, clearly knowing he was laying it on with a trowel. "Let's go," Jack said. "To tell the truth, I don't relish the thought of sleeping on that sofa tonight. I'd rather go to Boise, get a hotel near the airport, and take a morning flight home."

Skye raised her nose high. "I want separate rooms."

Jack grimaced. "Lady, I wouldn't have it any other way."

Skye went upstairs to get her bags while Jack called for an Uber driver. "Well, looks like I'm in luck. One will be in this area in 'only' thirty minutes. He had to drive to someplace called McCall and is now heading back to Boise."

"That's a break," Carly said.

"It is." Jack looked at Carly. "Take care of Alex while you're here. He's really a good man, but overwhelmed at the moment. And I do believe you're good for him."

It took close to forty minutes before the Uber driver arrived, but to Carly, it was well worth the wait. She had never felt so relieved to see the backs of two people.

Once they left, she locked up the house, keeping on a light in the foyer for Alex when he returned. And he would. If nothing else, to get his laptop and clothes.

As she looked back to make sure everything was in order before shutting off the lights in the great room, her gaze went to Elijah Donnelly's portrait.

He was smiling.

Smiling? She didn't get it. She thought he was on her side.

CHAPTER 23

Relief filled Carly at the sound of Alex and Hitchcock returning to the cabin about one a.m. After that, she slept peacefully until morning.

As Carly made preparations to cook Alex a breakfast of French toast, chicken-apple sausage, and a side of yogurt, granola, and berries, she reflected on the way he had talked about her disrupting his work the night before. If he really meant that, she would go after making his breakfast. It was the least she could do now that she realized how her presence may have hurt his career and to the money he was hoping to give to the children's home.

About ten a.m., he came downstairs, a sheepish expression on his face.

"You know—" she began.

"I want you to understand—" Alex said at the same time.

"You first," she said.

"I was just going to say I didn't mean *everything* I said last evening. I was angry and lashing out. Please stay."

Joy filled her. "You sure?"

"Really," he said. "After all, you're an owner of the cabin."

That wasn't the reason she had hoped to hear, but she'd take it. "I am, but you've put up with more than you should have. And you paid to have the cabin all to yourself."

"Your cooking is worth more than I'm paying, believe me. Stay. I know it's only for a few more days. And, I'll admit, I'll miss … more than your cooking when you're not here. I'll miss you."

No more than I'll miss being here. Being with you. The words filled her mind, but she didn't dare speak them aloud.

"Speaking of my cooking…" She quickly made breakfast for them both and, as they did in the days before Skye, Julia, and Jack invaded the cabin, they sat and ate together.

She'd been counting the days, and only three remained before she had to return to San Francisco, to her poor neglected business. Being here with Alex was an interlude in the natural course of her life, nothing more. An interlude with a creative and sensitive man that she would never forget. An interlude she would cherish in the days ahead.

She had three events scheduled for the upcoming week: two mid-week luncheons and a Saturday wedding reception.

None of them thrilled her. But at least it meant income, and that Carly's Catering wasn't dead. Yet.

She had failed in her goal of developing a plan to expand her business, but also, she had put little effort into it. A part of her was sorry that she had talked so much with Alex about studying botany, her love of flowers, and how she had always wanted to work with them. Resurrecting those forgotten dreams made her feel worse about her catering business than before she came to the cabin.

She could only hope that one of these days she would—as Jules constantly harped at her—feel happy that she had a business to call her own.

"You're being quiet," Alex said as he made himself another cup of coffee. He offered her more, but she shook her head.

"I was just thinking about all I haven't done while I've been here," she said, still seated at the counter, a little coffee left in her cup.

"You and me both." He took the barstool beside her. "Do you think you'll have time to hit your business books?"

"It doesn't matter." After a while she got up to rinse the dirty dishes and put them in the dishwasher. "Being here helped me with one thing. I now understand why I was having such trouble focusing. I don't really want a large, successful catering business. Is that terrible of me?"

"I'm not surprised—only surprised to hear you admit it." He spoke softly. "It seems to me you have no genuine passion for that business."

She gave him a baleful look. "It's true. But I suspect I'll just keep plugging away. Maybe find someone to handle the bookkeeping and somehow find the money to hire a full-time sous chef so I can concentrate on getting more events to cater, rather than trying to do everything myself."

"So you'll stick with it?"

"I've accepted it. Just as Julia said I should." She cleaned up the kitchen area. "Who am I to want more?"

"But you're..." He stopped.

"I'm what?"

He shook his head. "Who am I to advise? You see what a mess I've made of my own life."

It hurt to hear him talk that way. She understood why, but as his agent said, he dwelled too much on the past and past failures. "If you want to know what I see," she said, "it's a brilliant writer on the verge of huge success."

"You need to remove those rose-colored glasses."

"I don't think so," she said. "In fact, according to Jack, I may be doing the right thing here."

"What do you mean?"

She picked up a sponge and wiped down the island. "Jack

said he thought"—she paused and met Alex's eyes—"he thought I was a positive influence on you, on your writing. That seems odd, considering that you've hardly written anything at all around me."

He looked surprised. "He said that?"

"He also said you need time alone so you can write."

The kitchen clean, Carly was about to leave the room when Alex said, "I've got an idea. If I'm really not taking you away from your business books, would you have time to help me?"

She quickly replied, "Of course."

"Let's get some iced tea and sit out on the deck. I think … I think if I talk about my story with you, it might help. And since you do read some crime fiction…"

"Well, yes, you could say that," she admitted.

Alex told Carly he planned to open his thriller with Rip Tarrington on an airplane going to Dushanbe, once known as Stalinabad, the capital of Tajikistan. With that, he could launch into an explanation of the country's history.

"Hmm," Carly frowned. She sat on the bench, and he was on a rattan chair, their teas on the side table they shared.

Uh oh. "What's 'hmm' supposed to mean?" he asked.

"Well, I'm sure your loyal readers would stick with you if you opened with the side of a cereal box and they had to read all the ingredients. But they're looking for a Rip Tarrington super-spy story, and they want to know what Tarrington is up to right now. Who's with him? And since you're supposed to put a girl-friend in this book, why not open with him realizing he's tired of playing the field? I mean, the man has already proven he can get any woman he wants—married, single, young, old—so what's the challenge in that? Such 'relationships,' if you want to call them that, don't mean he's not lonely, or that he isn't looking for that someone special to have a deep, meaningful relationship with."

Alex listened, amazed, at all she knew about his lead character, until… "You've read my books!"

She swallowed. "Well, yes. I mean, I was curious."

His eyebrows lifted.

"Okay, I liked them," she said. "In fact, I couldn't put them down and went from one to the other. A major binge. So, I get it."

He felt his face, his whole being, slowly dissolve into an enormous smile. "You know," he murmured, "my own wife wouldn't read my books. She called them my 'little amusements.'"

Carly looked shocked and sorry. He saw that if anyone realized how much it had hurt him to have his wife so dismissive of something he loved and did so well, it would be Carly. He loved, correction, *liked*, her even more for such understanding.

"That's her loss," Carly said, and then took a sip of her tea. "And it doesn't make your work any less important to your fans. Rip is more than an action hero. He's a great guy. And all of us want to find out, in your next book, how well he's coping with the death of his best friend. I mean, he definitely got even with Hugo's killers, but now that the revenge is over, how is he handling the loss of the one guy who really understood him?"

"You've thought a lot about it," he murmured.

"Of course!"

"I thought you didn't like thrillers?"

Her face lit up in a smile. He loved it when she looked at him that way. "I thought I didn't either. But then I started reading thrillers written by this guy I'd never heard of named Alex Townson and discovered I couldn't put them down." She suddenly looked embarrassed. "When I was in town, I would go to the Rusty Nail or that little coffee shop with Internet service and download a book onto my e-reader. Then I'd read them, one after the other, while I was supposedly studying small business management up in my room."

The look on her face was priceless. He laughed—a loud, hearty laugh. "Thank you, Carly, for letting me know." A lot of people had read and enjoyed his books, but he felt especially pleased that she was one of them. "Is that why you stopped complaining about falling asleep in the afternoon?"

"You noticed?" Her gray eyes twinkled with delight and that lilac shade she claimed was 'impossible' appeared once more. "Well, I found them more interesting than the business books."

"I should hope so!" None of the women he'd dated since his divorce had read his books, and he never wanted them to read about Rip Tarrington. For one thing, they might expect he was like Rip—charming, sexy, and an exceptionally great lover—which he was sure would have resulted in some very disappointed dates.

"Back to your new story," she said, serious once more. "I want you to bring me into Rip's world as soon as you can. I'd be much happier to learn about Tajikistan along with Rip, through his eyes, rather than to feel like I'm reading a history book."

He rubbed his jaw. "The problem is because Rip is a former CIA officer, he already knows its history. There's not much more for him to learn. But the reader, I'm sure, doesn't have a clue about it."

She took his hand. "I hate to break it to you, Alex, but your readers just want to believe Rip knows and understands the place. I can see that you've researched the heck out of the subject and now you want to let everyone know every interesting tidbit you've found. I do want to learn *something* about the country. And I'm sure one reason people love your books is to learn about faraway places that they don't have a prayer of ever seeing. But let us experience it with Rip and his new girlfriend."

"I know that," he murmured as he reached for his tea. "It's

how I approached my last books. I don't know why it was such a stumbling block in this one."

She studied him a long moment before she said, "Could it be you just didn't want to take on Rip's love interest?"

"No way!" He put down the tea.

"If not that, what?"

His mind whirled with possibilities. "I'm sure there's something."

"Such as?"

"Maybe it's fear of success. I've heard that's a common ailment. My editor hopes this book will make the *New York Times* list. That's scary."

"Oh? And what if it doesn't?"

"That would be even worse."

"Ah! So it's not fear of making the *Times* list that's bothering you," she said, looking irritatingly smug.

Of course it is! He wanted to yell the words at her, even as he couldn't help but feel he would be lying to them both. He didn't like where this was going. "What else could it be?"

"I've already said what I think."

He got up and paced back and forth across the porch, then stopped and ran his fingers through his hair a couple of times before he got up nerve to tell her what she needed to understand about him. "Look, I didn't have the best experiences with women, okay. I spent most of high school skinny and nerdy. In the military, I traveled too much to form relationships. My first and only serious one was with Francine, and you've heard how that ended up. I was a dud husband and, I guess, an even worse boyfriend to hear women like Skye tell it. So how am I supposed to write a love story? I wouldn't know how to begin."

She nodded, her expression both understanding and forlorn. "I'm afraid I'm not a person to offer advice on that score."

"A great pair, aren't we?" he murmured, sitting down on the rattan chair once again.

She looked ready to agree, but then her demeanor changed. Head high, she got up and faced him, placing her hands on the arms of his chair and bending forward to look him in the eye. "You know what? Who cares? You're a writer. You've had Rip do all kinds of things you haven't done. So create for him a woman he can love. Make her up. Make her like no one you've ever been involved with. And then have him fall in love with her. As you write, think of me as your reader, a reader who's dying to get back into Rip Tarrington's world. Forget about some unknown person, like your editor, that you hope to impress with all your research and erudition. Just me. And I want, no, I demand, to be entertained *and* to feel how much Rip—funny, wise-cracking, tough-guy Rip—cares about this woman, or I'll put that book down faster than if it were yet another book on how to expand one's business."

He couldn't help but grin at how good her words made him feel. "I'll write the book for you." Saying the words aloud, they became a promise to her. A promise etched on his soul. Jack Bellar was right. She did inspire him. "I'll think of you wanting the pages to turn themselves as you read about Rip's latest adventures. In fact, I'm going to write you the best Rip Tarrington yarn you could ever imagine."

She straightened at those words and smiled at him. More than anything he would have liked to give her a quick, light kiss on the lips. A "thank you" kiss. But who was he kidding? He wanted more than that, and one kiss wouldn't be nearly enough.

He was so tempted … just try, his heart said. Kiss her. See how she reacts.

But she was returning to her life back in San Francisco; she had a business and responsibilities waiting for her back there. He had no business interfering with that. Not him. He seemed to disappoint people who got near him. Perhaps, as Francine and even Skye said, he just didn't know how to love.

And the last thing he could bear to do was to hurt Carly. He stood up.

"Time for me to go to work," he said, and then headed for the door into the great room.

"You'll let Rip fall in love," Carly called. "But will you let him stay with the woman?"

He stopped and thought for a moment. When the answer came, it hurt. Head bowed, he answered as honestly as he knew how. "I don't think so. Rip is a loner. I'm afraid that's the only kind of hero I could ever write about."

CHAPTER 24

Carly joined Alex for breakfast, but she wasn't hungry. She couldn't stop thinking about returning to San Francisco, returning to her business. The thought of going was a physical ache. She tried to tell herself it was because she didn't want to leave the cabin, but that was a lie. She didn't want to leave Alex. She'd done it—she'd opened her heart and now understood what people said when they used the term "broken hearted," because that was exactly how she was feeling.

Fortunately, Alex chattered on and on about his story, proud that he had written several thousand more words deep into the night.

He told her a little about what he had written, and she had to admit, it sounded like quite a thrilling adventure. She could almost see Rip Tarrington sleuthing out the bad guys as he raced through the dark, dangerous streets of Istanbul, and suddenly finding himself kidnapped and taken to the farthest reaches of Tajikistan where he had to save not only himself, but the attractive daughter of a U.S. ambassador.

She was glad Alex was so talkative since that stopped him from wondering why she was so quiet. Her stomach twisted and her head felt light at the terrible realization that going back to her home and business wasn't what she wanted at all. But her new dreams were unattainable, foolish, a dewy-eyed, impractical fantasy. It was imperative, *imperative,* that she not allow her reckless feelings for Alex Townson to upend everything she had worked to achieve—flawed and imperfect though it was.

She had to laugh at herself. She was acting more like a love-struck teenager than an adult businesswoman.

The love-struck part of her wanted to forget about her business, and to remain at the cabin for another couple of weeks to have a wild, romantic, once-in-a-lifetime fling with Alex.

She suspected he wouldn't say no.

But when their time was up and she returned to San Francisco, she would be catering for nobody because her business would have folded while she had been cavorting with the one man who actually made her heart go *zzzzing!*

And since, at her core, she was still a responsible businesswoman, she would leave Alex and go home.

It hurt.

On the other hand, she hadn't even known him two weeks. That was ridiculously short. She couldn't possibly be in love with him. He was a nice, interesting, fun-to-be-around, sexy, thoughtful fellow. But that didn't equate to love. Did it?

Anyway, she knew better than to trust in love. She had watched her own mother trust in love too much. Roxanne had cast aside first Julia's father, then Carly's, and even Mallory's because she thought the *next* man in her life would be her true love. And doing that, she had left chaos and three confused, unhappy children in her wake. Everything she did had been selfish, and Carly never forgave her for it.

Carly had vowed she would never act that way, would never care so little about others that she would hurt them for her own irresponsible desires. For that reason, she couldn't give up her father's business—the business he had worked all his life to build into something wonderful for her. She needed to care for it, nurture it. She had never walked away from responsibilities.

She wasn't about to start now.

She was not her mother's daughter.

She glanced up at Elijah Donnelly's portrait. When she was young and heard stories about people who had walked away from the love the cabin had found for them, she couldn't imagine anyone doing such a thing. Why in the world would anyone abandon love?

But now, she understood.

Romance was nowhere to be found on Carly's Catering menu.

***

Carly did the last bit of straightening up after breakfast and then poured herself a glass of iced tea. Alex was out on the back porch with Hitchcock but saw her through the French doors and waved at her to come out and join them.

"Don't worry," he said as she stepped onto the porch. "I'm still writing, so to speak. Come see." He held up a little black gizmo and then patted the spot beside him on the bench.

"What's that thing?" she asked as she sat.

"It's a digital recorder." Alex showed her. "My mind has been racing with this story, and since I can speak faster than I can type, I'm using a dictation program. It's speeding up the process like crazy."

She couldn't believe how excited he was. "That sounds great."

He was smiling, his eyes bright. "The bottom line is that my story is moving along faster than ever. I just might make Jack's deadline."

"Fantastic news. I'm happy for you."

"Thanks."

Conversation stopped and she could feel him looking at her as she petted Hitchcock, who was now sitting at her side.

"What's wrong, Carly?" he asked softly, putting down the recorder.

His words jarred. "Wrong?"

"You've been quiet all morning."

"I have?"

He placed his hands on his knees. "You leave on Sunday?"

"Yes."

His gaze was serious. "I don't suppose you could stay a little longer."

"I can't." She forced a smile and stared out at the orchard.

He watched her a long while, then took hold of her shoulders and made her face him. "Carly, is going back to San Francisco, back to your business, what you really want to do?"

She shut her eyes. She couldn't struggle with it any longer. "It's practical."

That seemed to take the wind out of him. He let her go, his jaw tight. "A practical idealist? Does that even make sense?"

He was the one not making sense. "Why do you keep insisting I'm an idealist? I told you, I'm not."

"But you are. Why else haven't you 'settled' into your job, or with that fellow of yours in San Francisco? Because deep down they aren't enough. They don't fill the passionate idealist you've tried hard to bury."

"I don't—"

"You've mentioned Julia's advice more than once," he said. "Julia's been more influential on you than you realize."

"No! She's—"

"Julia knows how great you are," he continued. "She might worry when you talk about abandoning your business, but that's because she's concerned about you. In you, I see a woman with ideals, and you've kept them even though you couldn't put them into practice. Not yet, anyway. That's a good thing, Carly."

Carly's shoulders slumped, her anger gone. "Isn't there an old saying that goes something like, 'a cynic is an idealist who's been kicked in the teeth by the world'? Maybe that's me."

"Is that how you're feeling now?"

She had no answer. All she knew was that she had no idea how this man—this relative stranger—could read what was in her heart so completely. There was so much she wanted to say to him, but she didn't dare. "I'm sorry," she whispered, turning to go.

"Stop. Please." He again reached for her, but she slipped past his grasp and went inside.

That evening, Alex went to the Rusty Nail.

Butch came by as soon as he sat. "Whiskey and water?" he asked.

Alex nodded. "Thanks."

"How's it going at the cabin?" Butch asked as he made the drink.

"I've seen things I simply can't explain," Alex said. It was hard to admit, but true. "I don't know what to think."

"Maybe the trick is to not think," Butch said. "But to accept. A lot that happens in this world that we can't explain. Maybe it's because science hasn't yet figured out the explanation, or maybe it's beyond the ability of the human mind to comprehend—sort of like the size of the universe."

"When did you become a philosopher, Butch?" Alex asked raising his glass in a salute to the bartender's words before taking a sip.

Butch chuckled. "When I took this job and began to listen to people—especially to those who came in here alone and were willing to talk about it, to tell me why they had no one with them."

Alex nodded. "Yes, we loners are a troubled lot."

"Not always," Butch said. "But the cabin's a unique place. Always has been. And it's probably never going to change. My advice? Enjoy it."

Alex couldn't help but smile. "You may well be right. And to start, I'll take a hamburger to go. I've got work to do."

CHAPTER 25

When Alex went downstairs the next morning after a long evening of writing, he expected to find Carly preparing his brunch, a cup of coffee by her side, and the delicious aroma of something baking in the oven wafting through the cabin.

But the kitchen was empty.

The cabin was so quiet he felt as if he could reach out and touch the silence. This was what his days here would be like once she returned to San Francisco. To her job.

He knew he shouldn't care, but he did. And he didn't know what to do about it.

Or was he just kidding himself?

Still, the way she had looked at him, touched him, danced with him, told him so much more than her words did. He wondered what might have happened between them if she were a freer spirit than she was. But then, she wouldn't be Carly.

He couldn't help but wonder, also, what might have happened between them if Julia, Skye, and Jack hadn't shown up. Maybe it was good that they had.

Carly wasn't a woman to take lightly. With her, it was all or nothing.

And although he knew that down to the marrow of his bones, he still wanted to be with her. But she was leaving, and he had to let her go. It was the best thing for them both. She needed someone who could love her completely, and he'd been told by good authorities that he didn't know how to love. So he would let Carly walk out of his life.

And he would return to Boston.

Carly walked into the cabin carrying two bags of groceries. Alex jumped up to help her.

"Have you changed your mind?" he asked, his tone hopeful. "Are you staying?"

"I've got events scheduled for the next week. But I bought some food for you, for when you're here alone. I wouldn't want you to starve, or get in a rut ordering pizzas every night if you're too busy writing to go into town to eat."

His face fell. "I see."

She began putting away the groceries. "I also realized that in all the time you've been here, I've never cooked you a really special meal. As a caterer, I've made some delicious dishes, and I wanted to make one for you as our last dinner together."

He froze. "What do you mean, last? Tomorrow's only Saturday. You have until Sunday, don't you?"

It took a moment before she could find her voice. "It'll take me all day Saturday to get home. Then, I'll have Sunday to get ready for work on Monday morning."

"But ..."

She turned away. Her emotions tugged too much at her heartstrings to look at him. "I'm afraid the longer I wait, the harder it'll be to go. This is for the best. Now, you go write. I have some preparation to do and I don't like people watching me as I cook."

"What are we having?"

"Cornish game hens with a mushroom and wild rice stuffing, asparagus with a curried mayonnaise dip, and an arugula salad with pecans, avocado and shaved Parmesan."

"You're going to cook all that alone?"

"It's not difficult. It just takes time. You'll love it."

"I imagine I will."

"I only ask one thing," she said.

He looked at her quizzically.

"We don't talk about tomorrow."

He nodded, his eyes sad. "While you're doing that, I'll make a quick run to the store to buy some wine."

She smiled. "No need to go that far. Cabernet sauvignon is in the car. Back seat."

"You've thought of everything."

She shrugged. "It's my job."

She said she'd do as much as she could as quickly as possible and get out of his way. He insisted that she wouldn't bother his writing, and that he actually liked having her near.

He didn't move from the great room as she cooked, and she found enough to do to linger in the kitchen longer than was actually necessary.

At six o'clock, dinner was ready.

One last time Alex moved his laptop and materials out of the way so that they could sit at the table for dinner. He found some candles in a drawer and lit them.

"Aren't you the romantic," Carly said.

He couldn't help but think if he were romantic, she wouldn't be leaving. He couldn't believe how much he hated that she was going. "It's the least I can do."

As she put the meal on the table, he expressed over and over how delicious everything looked and smelled.

He was about to say, "Your customers are lucky to have you," but that would ruin the warmth he felt, and he didn't want to do that. He wanted to do nothing to cause her to think of anyone but him that evening. So he took her hand and said a simple, "Thank you."

He opened the bottle of wine. "Would you like some?"

She lifted her glass for him to pour.

He took a bite of the Cornish hen. "Delicious. I've never had this before."

She smiled. "People say it tastes like chicken."

He grinned, knowing she was making a play on an old adage. "They say that about frogs legs, too."

"That's something I could never eat!"

He chuckled, but then fell into an awkward silence, only commenting on the different dishes she'd made and how good each one was. All he could think about was the fact that she was leaving the next day, and that was the last thing he wanted to talk about.

He'd already asked if she could stay longer, and she'd made it clear that wasn't an option. He couldn't imagine, however, the cabin without her in it.

Soon, dinner was over. As she began clearing the table, he went to the sink, turned on hot tap water and gathered the pots, pans, and oversized pieces to hand wash them.

She stared at him. "What are you doing?"

"I know how to wash pots and such," he said, reaching for the dishwashing liquid.

"But you're my guest."

"Not tonight. Tonight, we're not host and guest. We're just two people enjoying each other's company."

She smiled. "I like that."

"Me, too."

Soon, they took their coffee and went out to the back porch. They sat, side-by-side, on the bench. The night was balmy, and the moon nearly full.

"Another beautiful evening," he said.

"It is. In San Francisco, many nights the fog comes in and obscures even the moon. I can't tell you how much I enjoyed being here in summer as a child," she said. "The moon somehow seems bigger in summer. It would come up over the river, so big and white it seemed I should be able to reach out, grab it, and never let go."

"Did you come here often?"

"Only in summer," she began, then drew in her breath. With that, he realized that for all their talking, she told him very little about her childhood.

"Tell me about it," he murmured. "I'd like to know about those days."

She drew in her breath, and after a while, began to talk. "Summers were the only time my mother would bring me, Julia, and our younger sister, Mallory, to the cabin. We'd stay throughout July, sometimes arriving a little before, sometimes leaving a little after. Other than that, we each lived with our own fathers."

"Your *own* fathers?" She'd never indicated that she and her sisters had different fathers, although he'd wondered at how dissimilar she and Julia were, and their different last names.

"Yes. My mother apparently was missing a 'motherly' gene. And she'd be the first to admit it. I've never quite decided if she was also missing a 'wifely' gene or had too much of one because she ended up marrying at least four times that I know of. Each of her daughters went to live with our fathers after the divorce, as if Roxanne was rejecting not only her husbands, but the daughters they had sired. She and her fourth husband had no children. And after she married him, she no longer went to the cabin."

He shook his head. Although Carly relayed the story as if she were emotionless, even blasé, about her mother's rejection, he could only imagine how much it must have hurt her as a child. And he couldn't understand any mother giving up her children that way. "Why did she stop your get-togethers?"

She said nothing for a long time, but stared out in the direction of the orchard. Despite the bright moon, the orchard was dark and only the barest outline of the trees could be seen.

"I never knew for sure," she said finally. "I heard it might have been that her spouse at the time didn't want her to be around us. Eventually, she divorced him, too. And when she died, she was living alone. Where Roxanne is concerned, I have more questions than answers."

"How awful for you and your sisters." His heart ached for her. "I'm so sorry."

Carly sipped her coffee before she responded. "I'm just sorry I never got to know her better, or to understand her. Even at the cabin, she was more involved with her Garden Valley friends than her daughters. The three of us girls tried to hang around each other, but there's five years between each of us. We ended up being better friends with other kids our own ages in the area. Gunnar, who you met, was one of several kids Mallory and I used to play with up here. Julia seemed to think she was too old to play with her little sisters, but Mallory and I got along fine."

"At least that was a good thing," he said.

"It was," she agreed.

He reached for his coffee on the side table by the bench. It had gotten cold, so he just took a sip and put it aside. As he did that, a thought sprang to mind and he couldn't stop himself from saying, "It's also interesting that your mother married four times and, I'm guessing, you and your older sister haven't married at all."

"Ah, psychoanalyzing us, are you?" She gave him a wry grin.

"I am. What about the youngest, Mallory?"

She hesitated. "Oh, my. I'm not sure what you'll think about Mallory."

His eyebrows rose. "Why?"

"She's almost gotten married three times. Big engagements, big bridal showers, everything. But then she calls off the wedding shortly before it's supposed to happen. And one of those times, just as she was about to walk down the aisle."

"*Three* times?"

"That's right."

"Even more interesting," he murmured.

She shrugged. "Well, maybe someday I'll break the spell and get married."

The words landed like a dead balloon in his stomach. "Yes," he said, surprised at the bitter taste in his mouth as he said, "I imagine you will."

She must have heard something in his tone because her eyes widened a moment, then she dropped her gaze. "It's getting late. I'm going to try for an early start in the morning." She stood.

He stood as well. "Of course," he murmured, hating this.

She backed away. "Goodnight, Alex." With that, she hurried into the cabin.

Not until she was inside did he whisper, "Goodnight."

CHAPTER 26

When Carly came downstairs the next morning—her last morning at the cabin—she found Alex already up and dressed. Not only that, he had made coffee for himself, and put some on for her as soon as he saw her on the stairs. And he had covered the counter with bowls, utensils, flour, eggs, milk, butter, a sack of pecans, maple syrup, and a bunch of condiments.

"What are you doing?" she asked.

He placed a mug of coffee in front of her on the kitchen island. "I know how to make the world's moistest, fluffiest, maple-pecan pancakes. So I'm making breakfast for you." Then his brow wrinkled with worry. "You have time to eat before you leave, don't you?"

Her heart was aching at leaving, and at his thoughtfulness. "I've got time."

"Good." He poured her some orange juice. "Have a seat."

She did as told and soon discovered he was right—the pancakes were the best she had ever eaten. Unfortunately, she had no appetite, and the more she struggled with the thought of leaving him, the more her stomach knotted.

"No good?" he asked.

"They're wonderful," she whispered, striving to stop her voice from quavering. "You'll have to give me your recipe."

"Sure. I'll email it to you."

She nodded. Soon, she saw that after a few bites, he, too, pushed his dish away.

"I should get going," she said.

"I guess so." He stood and saw her suitcase in the foyer. "Let me help you. And grab some water for your trip. And maybe a sandwich. Or two."

She smiled at the sudden burst of Alex-as-mother-hen and took a couple of waters. "I'll be fine."

He carried the suitcase out to her car. "Where's Hitchcock? I thought he'd be here to see you off."

"I thought so, too." She looked around.

Alex and Carly called him, but when he didn't show up, Alex went into the house to see if he was there, then into the back-yard. "I can't find his leash," Alex said, his brow furrowed when he returned to her.

"When did you last use it?" Carly asked.

"This morning, but I'm sure I took it off after his walk. I just don't know where he is." Alex looked worried. "He never wanders off alone."

"This makes no sense," Carly stated.

"Well, you should get going. I'm sure he's okay."

"I can't leave worrying about him," she said. "Do you think he might have gone down to the river?"

"It's possible," he said.

"Julia told me we have a neighbor. Maybe Hitchcock went off with him."

"A neighbor? Where? I haven't even seen a house nearby, let alone people. I doubt that's it."

"We need to find him," she said.

He nodded, then he took her hand. Without saying a word,

except to call Hitchcock's name every few minutes, their steps turned toward the river. They had almost reached the spot near the water where Skye did her water nymph routine when they saw Hitchcock splashing in the river. As soon as he saw them, he ran to them, looking wet and happy.

"Oh, no!" Alex cried. "He took himself for a swim. I hope that isn't a new trick he's learned."

Carly noticed his leash had been clipped to his collar. "Look." She pointed to it.

"How…?" Alex's eyes showed his confusion. "I guess I forgot to unhook it in my eagerness to cook breakfast. Maybe with it on, he figured it's walk time."

"Maybe," she said dubiously. She found it hard to imagine not noticing Hitchcock dragging his leash through the house all morning. The ghosts—if there were such things—had been quiet since Skye left, and they certainly provided another explanation for Hitchcock's behavior. But this wasn't the time to go there.

"I can't say I'm sorry to be here at the river with you one last time," Alex said, intertwining his fingers with hers once more. "I love it here."

So did she, even as she noticed that, in the past, Alex always had a reason to take her hand, but this time, it was for no reason —or possibly, the best reason of all. Hand-in-hand, he pointed out four elk grazing on the far side of the river.

"Seeing elk is a sign of good luck," he said.

"Really? I've never heard that." She remembered the first time they came here and saw the elk. Her hand tightened on his.

"Well, I hope it's true, because I need all the luck I can get."

"You seem to make your own luck," she said with a gentle smile. "And that's the best kind."

He drew in his breath. "Is it? Or is it you? Your calm presence, your enthusiasm. Maybe it's because I'm with you that I've written as much as I have these past few days."

Her heart pounded. "I doubt that."

"I don't."

She shook her head. "You can write whether I'm here or not, and you will because it's what you do. What you love. Trust me on that."

His eyes softened. "If you say so." His voice was a whisper.

She thought about telling him she wanted to stay with him, telling him not only how she felt about him, but that she was willing to give up her business and do whatever it took to be with him.

But she wasn't that brave. Or that reckless.

Scarcely able to hold herself together, she murmured, "I should leave now. I have a very long drive ahead of me."

He nodded, and they walked, still holding hands, to the cabin, Hitchcock following.

"Since the car is already loaded, I don't have to go back inside," she murmured. And I couldn't bear to, she thought. "So I'll just say goodbye here." Reluctantly, she let him go.

"Sure. I understand."

She opened the driver's door to get in. He took her arm, turning her to face him. "It's been a pleasure getting to know you, Miss Carly Fullerton," he said. "I'm going to miss you."

"I'll miss you, too, Alex."

He put his arms around her. Their eyes met, but she began to pull away from him. She couldn't kiss him or let him kiss her. That would make it too hard to leave him, or to forget him. She knew his kisses were far too tempting. But his arms tightened just enough to stop her.

As he leaned closer, her arms circled his back. And then his lips met hers ... just long enough for her to recognize it was much more than a friendly kiss. He lifted his head, and she smiled ... just enough of a smile for him to know she found his kiss every bit as amorous as she had known it would be.

But then her arms tightened, and she kissed him back,

longer, more intensely, and equally heartbreaking. He pulled her close, holding her hard against his chest and returning her kisses with the same fervor she gave them.

Soon, she had no choice but to let him go, or it would have been impossible to leave him. And she couldn't do that—not to him, not to herself. She quickly got into the car.

He took hold of the door. "Carly—"

"Don't!" she pleaded, fighting back tears.

His eyes searched her face a long moment, then he nodded.

"Goodbye, Alex," she murmured. "Write to me, and let me know how you're doing with your book, okay?"

He forced a small smile. "Okay. And I'll send you that recipe."

"You do that. And don't let the ghosts bother you!"

His eyes were sad even as his smile broadened. "No way."

He shut the door for her. She quickly started the engine and as she backed out of the driveway, she let her tears fall.

CHAPTER 27

Dom Delucci and his staff had cleared out of Carly's kitchen when she arrived back in San Francisco on Saturday night. The kitchen appeared no worse for wear.

On Sunday, she did all kinds of practical things like grocery shopping, laundry, picking up her mail, and making a list of all she'd need to buy for her business next week. She then called the two people she most often used when she had a job too big to handle alone and asked if they were available to help her at two of her events the upcoming week.

They were available and sounded happy to have her back. She was glad, yet hated that she couldn't return their enthusiasm. It was wrong of her, and she knew it. They were good kitchen assistants and genuinely decent people. Too good and decent to be stuck with a half-hearted employer who couldn't even offer them permanent jobs. They deserved better.

By late afternoon, weary, she went into the little one-room "apartment" behind her commercial kitchen and sat in her favorite easy chair, one that had been her father's. Oddly— perhaps because she'd spoken so much to Alex about Roxanne—

her thoughts turned to her mother. She had spent her life believing Roxanne had left her husbands and daughters because she thought they weren't good enough for her. But what if Roxanne actually felt the opposite?

She knew Roxanne had been frustrated by her career, that despite the praise she received, she never rose as high as she thought she should. Roxanne had a glorious voice, but she was missing something, some intangible charisma, and her career had stalled. That had to have been a bitter pill for her, perhaps even a key to her unhappiness and disappointment. Her sense of failure.

Carly wondered if Roxanne hadn't turned to love to cure that unhappiness, as if believing the right "lover" could be the key to opening up other avenues of success for her. But no matter how hard she tried, how many men she thought she was in love with, or married, or had affairs with, it didn't change the bottom line: it didn't change *her*. She was still Roxanne with talent … but not enough talent to fulfill her dreams.

She had thrown herself into her career to the detriment of her own family. What if guilt had plagued her? What if she recognized that such selfishness was ultimately wrong, and could be destructive?

What if Roxanne felt about her family the way Carly now did about her two kitchen assistants—that she wasn't quite good enough for them? To feel that about employees was bad, but how much worse would it be to feel that way about one's own family, one's own children? Was that why Roxanne could scarcely bear to face her children after having walked out on their fathers? And she continued unable to face them except for one month each summer until that, too, caused her too much guilt to continue?

With those thoughts, whether correct or not, the veil that had shrouded her mother lifted. Carly realized her father hadn't caused Roxanne's problems, nor had Julia's, or Mallory's. And

Roxanne's three daughters definitely hadn't. Instead, the problems were Roxanne's, and only Roxanne's—her inability to accept her own abilities and limitations, and to find happiness with what she had, rather than misery and resentment over what she couldn't attain.

The years of anguish and unhappiness Carly had spent trying to understand what she had done to cause her mother to reject her at such a young age swept over her as she realized Roxanne's treatment of her had nothing to do with her actions.

And now, Carly's only feeling was one of regret for the years she'd never had with her mother, for the summers they should have spent at the cabin but didn't, and regret that Roxanne had three fine daughters that she had never really gotten to know. She shook her head with pity.

But more than anything, it was time to move on from all that. To get on with life. Her life.

Her two weeks at the cabin had given her a taste of what living a life filled with love might have been.

A part of her wondered if she might have been happier if she had never discovered what it felt like to look at a man and feel her heart become so full it might burst from sheer joy, or that a simple smile could blot out the sun because it shined so much more brightly.

Maybe she was feeling a weird "cabin fever." Even to her—practical and realistic "idealist" that she was—for two weeks the cabin had seemed the most idyllic, magical place on earth.

She wondered if any new man in her life could ever compete with what she had found there. Although, if the tale about the ghosts was correct, since she had turned her back on the true love they had found for her, she was doomed to never find another.

CHAPTER 28

Alex felt miserable, more miserable than he ever been in his life. He had no appetite, and a listlessness that felt as if the weight of the world was on his shoulders. He decided he must be coming down with an illness—the flu, perhaps. What else could possibly be wrong with him?

The day before, he had watched Carly drive away, and when he went back into the cabin, it felt hollow as a tomb. His gaze turned to the kitchen where he had so often watched her efficiently prepare the best breakfasts and dinners he'd ever eaten. The back porch where they'd spent many an evening gazing at the stars. The sofa where they'd sit and talk in the evening, sometimes listening to old musicals.

Old musicals… He remembered how teary-eyed she'd become listening to "If I Loved You," and how they had danced to it. What if he'd been brave enough to tell her how he felt? To ask her to stay with him?

How did he let her go without saying what was in his heart?

But he felt he had no choice. He was being … practical. Like Carly. They were too different, lived too far apart, in different worlds. After all, he'd only known her two weeks. It was madness to think he could fall in love after only two weeks. Wasn't it?

Yet, he knew in his heart how she felt about him—she wore her emotions on her sleeve, and he loved that about her. And well he knew how he felt about her. Didn't they deserve to at least try to make it work?

Everything in his life had taught him it never would. But Carly was like no one who had ever been in his life. Amazingly, she seemed to understand him. To understand his books, and why he needed to write them. To understand the solitude he needed, and when he needed a break from too much quiet. He'd never met anyone like her.

But he had let her drive away without saying a word. Now, he sat in front of his computer, his heart so heavy with anguish he didn't know why he bothered to try to write anything sensible.

He watched the minutes, then the hours tick by, but he wouldn't leave his computer until he did what he had come here for. It would be nice *not* to fail at something, and that meant giving Jack a draft. He doubted it would be a draft that anyone would want to read, but at this point, he scarcely cared. He pretty much had the bones of the story down, and the bones were good, but the story was desperately missing something— some spark; some excitement. He was pushing, trying to force excitement into the manuscript, but it just wasn't happening.

At this point, he would have even accepted some ghostly interference!

He'd never figured out what exactly was going on at the cabin, but, of course, it wasn't ghosts. Everything—almost—had an explanation. And those things he couldn't explain were simply because he hadn't yet figured out, logically, how they'd happened. Nothing more was going on here.

The wind blew louder and stronger than ever before. He stepped out onto the back porch. The moon and stars slowly vanished as darkening clouds carrying the storm blew closer. He heard the trees bending in the wind and heard the rattle of the windows of the house. In the distance, a tree limb snapped.

He went back indoors and had just sat down at his computer when the electricity went out.

He remembered there were candles in the kitchen and used his phone's flashlight to find them.

There were tall taper candles, and smaller votive ones. He chose the votive size and put one on the plate on the kitchen island, and another beside his computer. No electricity should give him an opportunity to write since there was nothing else for him to do. His laptop had switched over to battery power.

He sat hoping for some unique idea, some clever plot line, to give his story the glow and passion it lacked. But his mind was as blank as ever, and his eyes kept wanting to shut. He refused to allow himself to sleep while candles burned in the cabin. His head nodded a few times, but he managed to jerk himself awake.

Once again it happened, but this time, when he made himself open his eyes, he jumped off his chair and backpedaled.

Facing him, with a palm resting on the dining table, while the knuckles of his other hand were pressed against his hip, stood the spitting image of Elijah Donnelly, even to the point of wearing Elijah's old-fashioned clothes. "Ah! He wakes!"

"Who are you?" Alex cried. "How did you get in here?"

Alex glanced over at Hitchcock, who was looking at the stranger as if he knew him, and didn't seem at all troubled by his presence.

Elijah straightened. "You know who I am."

"No. I must still be sleeping and don't realize it." Alex's voice trembled.

"Is that what you truly think?" With his hands clasped behind his back, Elijah paced back and forth in front of Alex. "Sit at your computer again, why don't you? That's what you do best, after all. Not that you accomplish much of anything there, except to hide from your life."

Alex picked up a candle and marched across the room to the fireplace. He held it up high to illuminate the portrait. The background was there, but Elijah Donnelly wasn't. *No! Impossible!*

"This is ridiculous," Alex muttered, and threw himself back into the chair by his computer. "Now I know I'm dreaming. I only wish I could write stories half as outlandish as this dream!"

"You might be dreaming. Who is to know? But it *is* time for you to wake up, boy," Elijah thundered. "You are one sorry fellow to let the best thing that ever happened to you walk out of your life."

Alex smarted at the word "boy," but immediately let it slide as Elijah's other words echoed his earlier thoughts. "She's better off this way," he said.

"Oh? It's for you to decide what's better for her, is it? And here I thought men and women in this century had gotten past such patriarchal attitudes."

"I'm not being patriarchal. I don't know that she feels as strongly as I do. And she's got a business and a life in San Francisco. And … I don't know what to say to her."

"Boy," Elijah bent low and looked him directly in the eyes. "You're a writer, so write! Her reaction will tell you everything you need to know."

Alex shut his eyes as he shook his head. "It's just not that easy." He opened his eyes again to explain himself further to Elijah, strange though it was to try to explain anything to a ghost.

But Elijah was gone.

And even stranger, an idea burst into his head for his book. A great idea. And all of a sudden, he knew exactly what he needed to write.

The evening after catering a wedding on Saturday, Carly received a text from Alex. A week had passed since she had left the cabin.

—The phone and internet here are now even worse than before you left. But here's a link to the pancake recipe I promised. I confess I stretched the truth a tad. It's not my creation. Maybe that's why it's so delicious. How are you doing?

She couldn't believe how relieved she felt to finally hear from him. For the past week, she'd wondered why he hadn't written or called. Had he forgotten her that quickly? But maybe he was concentrating on his book. He sounded well, and his few words were upbeat. All she knew was that his text—despite saying nothing personal—had brightened her day beyond belief.

—All is well here. Same as ever. Keeping busy. But I miss the cabin!

—Cabin misses you, too. Lots of strange noises. Keeps me awake at night, but since that's when I write, it's all good.

—I'm glad. Keep writing!

She checked her phone every few minutes to see if he had replied, but he hadn't.

Eventually, she stopped looking.

The next week she lined up two additional business luncheons. It wasn't fantastic, but better than nothing. Then, on Thursday, she received a desperate phone call from an event planner.

"One of San Francisco's longest serving supervisors will turn seventy on Sunday, and we planned a massive party. But the caterer and most of her staff are all sick! Can you take it on? We'll pay double your usual fee. The menu is all figured out. I just need someone who can cook!"

"Calm down," Carly said. "Unless the dishes are very exotic, my staff and I should be able to handle them. Where can we meet to go over the menu?"

Carly and the planner met and determined she could handle the job. It wouldn't be easy, and she would need to bring on most of the people on her roster of kitchen assistants and sous-chefs to take part and work just about around the clock, but at double her usual price, it was well worth the effort. And Carly was glad for the work. She found that the only way to stop thinking about Alex was to throw herself into each task harder than ever and to concentrate on making every item on her menu as delicious and attractive as she could.

That same evening, she heard the "ding" of a text message. Her suppliers had discovered she responded to texts faster than emails, and used them more and more often, so it took a while before she had a break in her cooking and looked at her phone. But when she did, her heart leaped.

—I finish the draft! I think Jack will be happy. I'll wait here until I get a thumbs up or thumbs down from him. I'd rather make revisions here at the cabin than back in Boston. Something about being here made the story easy to write. Wish me luck!

—I'm so very glad to hear you've finished. I'm sure Jack will love it. Now you can enjoy the area for a few days before heading back East. I hope you remember the places I suggested that are worth seeing.

—I remember everything you ever told me.

—I should hope so!

She was sure he'd respond to such blatant self-aggrandizement, but he didn't. She kept waiting, hoping. But nothing.

On Saturday, in the midst of her preparations for the big Sunday birthday gala, she heard back.

—Jack loved it. Said it was even better than he'd hoped. I'd like to send you a copy of the draft. You've been such a big help to me, I don't want you to have to wait until the book is printed and all—that'll take forever. Send me your address and I'll ship you a copy.

She stopped working on the humongous and ever-expanding arrangements long enough to send Alex a quick congratulatory message along with her address. She then wished him a safe trip back home.

He hadn't said he was going back to Boston, but earlier he had told her he'd wait in Idaho in case he had to make any revisions, and since he didn't need to …

It surprised her that he mentioned nothing about leaving Idaho, or about the cabin, or even about her. She guessed she'd been right all along. That staying at the cabin, meeting her, their long conversations, hunting for ghosts, listening to Roxanne's voice as she sang romantic songs from old Broadway musicals, hiking along the river banks, and every other strange, fun thing that had happened while they were there together, had all been a happy diversion for him. An "amusement" as his ex-wife would have said.

And it was now over.

The day of the big birthday bash finally arrived, and Carly was up at five a.m. to make sure everything was ready. Working on it, she only thought about Alex 75% of the time, instead of 99%.

She had received no response from him after sending the text with her address.

The setting for the party was the lovely Waterfront Club at Fisherman's Wharf. It had enough room to fit the two-hundred fifty invited guests. When Carly had learned the size of the gathering and the variety of fancy hors d'oeuvres selected, she had understood why the prior caterer and her staff had suddenly become ill. But for Carly, the money involved had made it worth working twenty-four-hour days.

She brought in floral arrangements for the buffet tables, using gerbera daisies in a multitude of colors. They were bright, happy flowers, befitting a birthday. Into each arrangement, Carly had tucked one small syringa flower. She doubted anyone would even notice the tiny white petals, but they meant a lot to her.

Carly's hors d'oeuvres, both hot and cold, along with elaborate fruit and dessert platters including individual pies, tortes, tarts, cakes, and custards, were so well liked people kept coming back for seconds and thirds. Carly was ecstatic by the many compliments she received about the food and its presentation, and several people requested her business card. The events planner informed her that Carly's Catering was now her go-to caterer.

When people started dancing, the catering crew removed all but the desserts and beverage services. As Carly helped, she also enjoyed listening to the music.

Most of the crowd was older, and the music was as well. A woman with a beautiful operatic voice sang several romantic show tunes. "I Could Have Danced All Night" from *My Fair Lady* brought nearly everyone onto the dance floor.

As Carly listened to the song, memories of being at the cabin, listening to old show tunes, and dancing with Alex, filled her heart.

But when the next song, "If I Loved You," began, it was all

she could do to hold it together. She quickly loaded a tray with dirty dishes, and carried it off to the kitchen. There she remained until the party was over and she could go home.

When Carly returned to her commercial kitchen, she was astounded to find a package had been delivered. Alex had not only overnighted his manuscript to her, but he'd set it up for Sunday delivery.

Several kitchen assistants had returned with her to bring back the equipment and clean everything up after the incredible event they'd pulled off. They all were exhausted but happy. The party had been a huge success.

Still, Carly could hardly wait to be alone so that she could open Alex's manuscript.

As soon as everyone had gone, she went into her little studio in the back of the commercial kitchen, and changed into lounging pajamas. She'd eaten enough of the leftovers from the party that she wasn't hungry. She was beyond exhausted, but knew she couldn't sleep if she didn't read at least the first chapter of Alex's story.

From the first paragraph, she could tell he was on fire. This book was going to be a great adventure, fun, and exciting to read. The first chapter began much as they had discussed—a rip-roaring, guns-blazing, action-packed opening in which the bad guys captured Rip, and he ended up badly beaten and convinced they would torture and kill him.

"Ah, Rip, you poor thing! You should know by now, you'll survive," Carly said, smiling. She put down the manuscript. She'd never admit it to Alex, but she was too tired to read that night after having worked all day on only three hours sleep.

Maybe tomorrow …

CHAPTER 30

The next morning, Carly again had to get up at the crack of dawn to prepare food for a small business brunch. It didn't pay much, but it was a job. Maybe Carly's Catering would survive after all. She should be glad. *"Should"* be ...

And that, she realized, was the problem.

By late afternoon, the event completed, and alone in her room, Carly did something she had never dreamed she would do.

She phoned Dom Delucci. He'd been ecstatic over having had the use of two commercial kitchens. She asked if he'd like to have the second kitchen permanently, and with it, she had two outstanding assistants looking for full-time jobs.

He jumped at the chance. Carly had a price in mind, a price that would help her establish a nursery in or near Boise, Idaho. They dickered a bit and soon came to an agreement.

For the first time in years, Carly found herself looking forward to what the future might bring. It was scary, but exciting. And oddly, even though she realized she was taking on a new, difficult venture that could result in utter and complete failure, she felt … happy.

She changed into comfortable clothes, made herself a cup of coffee, and sat down in her favorite easy chair with Alex's manuscript in hand.

Rip Tarrington had found himself targeted by a group of terrorists who hated him and everything he and the CIA he once worked for represented. They kidnapped him and the daughter of the U.S. Ambassador to Turkey and spirited them to Tajikistan.

The kidnappers threatened to kill them both if the U.S. government refused to pay a two-hundred million dollar ransom.

Rip and the woman were bound and gagged and tossed into a dungeon. There, Rip scraped the zip tie that bound his hands against a protrusion on the rough stone of the walls, and then snapped the tie apart, freeing his hands. He tore the bandanna from his eyes, yanked the tape off his mouth, and pulled out the tiny razor he kept in the heel of his boot. Using it, he slashed the zip ties at his ankles, then crawled over to the woman.

"It'll be all right," he whispered. "I'll get us out of here."

He lifted the bandanna from her eyes and to his surprise, instead of the brown eyes of the ambassador's daughter, this woman had gray eyes. Large, beautiful eyes that were scared, but looked at him as if he embodied every ounce of hope she had in the world. "This will hurt," he said, loosening a corner of the wide tape that covered her mouth. "Try your best not to cry out."

She nodded, and he ripped the tape from her face. He saw tears come to her eyes from it, and more than anything he wanted to kiss those tears away. He used the razor to slice the zip ties on her wrists and ankles and then helped her sit up.

She had red hair, just like the ambassador's daughter, but she wasn't her. Of that, Rip was glad, because the ambassador's daughter was such a shrew that he was initially tempted to leave her tied up and lying on the stone floor. But somehow, in just those first few moments, he could tell that this woman was kind and gentle. And gorgeous.

"Who are you?" he asked.

"Harly Orchid," she whispered. Her voice was soft and husky. And her body had generous curves in all the right places.

When he found his voice again, he asked, "Why are you here?"

"I have no idea," she said. "I'm nothing but an events planner. The Ambassador hired me to plan his wife's birthday party. It's next week, and I was at his house working on some details when the terrorists broke through the barricades. They started shooting, and I ran up the stairs, trying to hide. I crawled under a bed, but they found me. I don't know why they captured me and brought me here."

"Who's room were you in?" Rip asked.

"I'm not sure. I think it may have been the ambassador's daughter's."

"His daughter ... yes, that must be who they think you are. You both have red hair, although hers is more auburn and thin, while yours is fiery and lush. Obviously, they don't know what she looks like or they'd never have taken you. But now, you've got to keep them thinking you're Caroline, or they might kill you like they did everyone else working in the ambassador's house that day."

"Oh, no!" she cried.

He put his arms around her, surprised to discover how good it felt to hold her. "Don't worry. I'll get us out of here. They'll be sorry they ever messed with Rip Tarrington."

"Oh, Rip! How can I ever thank you?"

"We'll find a way."

Carly put the manuscript down at that point and laughed. "Alex, you stinker!" She couldn't get over him writing her into his story like that. The entire thing was beyond fun, especially since she knew that despite Rip's lascivious way of thinking about "Harly the events planner," he would fall in love with her.

"Well," Carly said aloud, "I hope Rip Tarrington and Harly Orchid have better luck getting together than Alex Townson and Carly Fullerton ever did."

She picked up the manuscript. This was definitely a story she could not put down.

When she reached the end, she was both laughing and crying. Rip did nothing half-way, and after saving the girl and himself, he asked her to climb to the top of Kilimanjaro in Africa with him. She did it.

"Any woman who'd climb this cold, icy rock with me has to be the best woman in the world. I love you, Harly Orchid. Will you marry me?"

"Oh, Rip. After you, how could I ever look at another man?" And as she said that, he noticed that her eyes turned from gray to the most beautiful shade of lavender he had ever seen. It wasn't the first time he saw them change color. They did that whenever she looked at him with love. Because of that, even before she said the words, he knew what her answer would be.

"Yes, I'll marry you."

He took her in his arms and made such passionate love to her, that they melted a spot on the icy ground, a spot that perfectly fit their forms as they held each other in their arms and vowed to cherish and love each other forevermore.

The End

"Oh, Alex," she murmured, her heart full. There was still one more page left, and she wondered why. After all, the story had ended.

She turned to that last page. It had only one line:

I dedicate this book to C. F., who taught me how to love.

CHAPTER 31

Before dawn the next morning, Carly phoned Julia. Thankfully, she answered the phone this time.

"Jules, do you have Alex's address back in Boston in the paperwork he filled out?"

"And hello to you, too. How are you? Me, I'm fine. Thanks for asking."

"Hilarious, but I've got to know." Carly was all but shouting into the phone.

"Why?"

"It's important. I need to see him. Face-to-face."

"Well, in that case you don't want to go to Boston. He extended his stay at the cabin. He's there another two weeks."

Carly gasped. She could hardly believe it. "Jules, I love you! Talk to you later."

"Wait! What—?"

As she neared the cabin, the radio—before it went all staticky—was playing an old show tune, "Tonight" from *West Side Story*. It couldn't have been more perfect.

The sun was setting as she turned onto the cabin's driveway. She didn't see Alex's car. Could Jules have been wrong? But he often parked it in the garage.

She got out of the car and to her relief saw Hitchcock at the window. That meant Alex was there, or would return soon.

Her legs wobbled nervously and she could scarcely walk.

She had only taken a couple of steps when the front door opened.

Alex stood in the doorway. They said nothing a long moment until Alex broke the silence. "I can't believe you're here."

Her pulse was doing a samba as she continued toward him. "How could I stay away after reading your story? It was beautiful."

He walked onto the driveway, then stopped. "After I sent you the manuscript, I kept waiting for a phone call or text. Sitting here alone, I was half the time scared and the other half hopeful over what your reaction to *Rip in Love* might be. But I never thought you'd come here."

She also stopped. "It made me laugh at times, and other times it brought me to tears. I loved it."

With that, he hurried until he stood right in front of her, then stopped, his green eyes smoldering and intense. "You taught me what to say, and how to say it—and you didn't even know it. Your silences forced me to think about how I felt so I could put those feelings into words. I hope I did you justice."

"More than that," she whispered.

"Everything I said was true."

She couldn't stop herself from reaching for him. Her hands went to his shoulders. "I'm glad."

He held her waist. "I can write anywhere as long as you're

with me. And judging from my agent's and editor's reaction to Harly Orchid, I might need to study you even more than I have already to make her character come even more alive."

Her eyebrows rose, and she smiled. "So you just want to use me?"

He grinned. "In many ways, in fact."

She couldn't help but laugh. "Uh, oh. You're sounding like Rip."

"Birds of a feather, I guess." He touched the side of her face, his fingers a gentle caress. "Would you like it if I went with you to San Francisco?"

She shook her head. "I sold Carly's Catering. It was time. I decided to take the money and use it to open a nursery."

He looked stunned. "Really? You did that?"

"Someone told me it's important in life to try to do what you love," she said. "It's good advice, and I'm going to take it."

"And where do you want your nursery?" he asked, his gaze searching her face. "Maybe here? The way we once discussed?"

He sounded so happy as he asked his questions, it gave her hope as she replied, "I can't think of anyplace better."

"I'm glad to hear it," Alex admitted. "It's perfect. Except for one thing."

"What's that?"

He suddenly gave her a quick kiss, as if he couldn't *not* kiss her, but he didn't dare, as yet, to make it passionate. But then he took her hand and led her into the cabin to stand in front of the picture of Elijah Donnelly. "I really don't believe in ghosts," Alex announced.

Carly's eyebrows rose. That was the last thing she was expecting to hear.

"And," he continued, "everything that happened probably was simply because I was in the cabin alone and concentrating hard."

She had no idea what he was talking about, but she said simply, "Yes?"

"All I know is, this is the place we need to be right now."

Carly nodded as she glanced from Alex to Elijah to Alex again. Elijah's expression was non-committal.

"I love you, Carly," Alex said. "From the moment I first saw you looking both scared and defiant, I knew there was something special about you. And as I got to know you, that feeling turned to love." He reached into his pocket and held out a small velvet box. "I saw this and bought it hoping, praying, you might feel the same." He dropped to one knee. "Will you do me the honor of becoming my wife?"

She was stunned. Rip had said that, but Alex? She took the box and opened it. The diamond ring was beautiful. "My God, Alex."

"Your eyes are the most beautiful shade of lilac I've ever seen." He stood. "Does that mean it's a yes?"

"Yes!" She let him slip the ring on her finger, then put her arms around his neck. "I love you, Alex!"

He kissed her. Finally, a loving, long, passionate kiss that went on and on and was returned by her many times over.

And Elijah smiled.

CHAPTER 32

The next morning, Alex wanted to take Carly out to a fantastic brunch somewhere in Boise where they could then apply for a license, and marry as soon as possible. Just the two of them. Alex suggested that they'd waited long enough. After all, they had "lived together," as he put it, for two entire weeks. Why wait?

Carly couldn't help but agree. He was all she ever wanted or needed.

"Are we crazy?" Carly asked as she got into Alex's car. "What will people back in Boston say?"

"That I'm a lucky fellow. All I know is I'm happy, and I want to be with you forever."

"Forever," Carly whispered.

As Alex backed out of the driveway, her gaze drifted over her beloved cabin, a place filled with love—and possibly more than a little magic. In the window of the river-view room, she noticed movement.

She leaned forward. The movement startled her and had her wondering if she might have left some window open, causing a breeze. She looked more closely.

Although she would never admit it to anyone, she saw three figures holding hands, as if they were a family. The first was a man with blond hair, a gray suit, and a white carnation in his lapel. Carly stared, unbelieving, the skin on her head and arms tingling because she knew exactly who that was. Beside him was a petite woman with dark brown hair parted in the middle and pulled back tight. She wore a calico dress with a high collar. On her other side stood a taller man, with thick brown hair and broad shoulders, wearing an off-white muslin shirt and brown slacks. Carly gasped. He looked much like the man she had seen on the driveway giving Julia flowers.

"Oh, my," she murmured, and glanced at Alex.

"What's wrong?" he asked.

But when she looked back, they had vanished.

She sat quietly, contemplating what had just happened. But soon, a broad smile filled her face. "I was just thinking how very happy I am."

He grinned. "Me, too," he said, giving her hand a quick squeeze as he headed toward the highway.

Her heart was full and warm as she thought of the three in the window. She hoped this strange existence of theirs was bringing them some kind of happiness, because they, and the cabin, had brought her more than she had ever dreamed possible.

PLUS ...

CHAPTER 1

Mallory Conway logged out of the Piaget Realty network and checked the clock on her laptop: 6:12 PM. She was at home in a postage-stamp size apartment in midtown Manhattan, a place she could afford only because she was subletting it from one of her boss's clients.

She had forty-five minutes to get ready for tonight's date, but first she had a deadline to meet for her other job.

Her secret job.

By day she was a listing assistant for residential properties at an exclusive Manhattan realty office, but by night she turned into Dear Nellie, columnist for the lovelorn.

The column had begun as a lark.

Seven months earlier, the editor of the *Greenwich Village*

Gazette, Brian Abernathy, a tall, pudgy, middle-aged man, happened to be a Piaget client looking for a condominium to purchase. One day, he showed up at the realty office and said he would need to put aside finding a new condo for a while. His current "advice" columnist had been arrested for embezzlement, and the column was the paper's most popular feature. Without it, fewer people would look past page one, which meant fewer advertisers, and that meant less revenue for the paper and less income for him. So he had to find a replacement quickly.

"What kind of advice column is it?" Tom Campilongo, Piaget's top broker, had asked.

"Relationships, what else?" Abernathy had replied. "The 'should I stay with my spouse even though he drinks and beats me?' kind. And the 'does my boyfriend love me when he still goes out with his former fiancée but swears they're just good friends?' questions." The two men laughed.

Hardy har har, Mallory had thought. She sat quietly hidden away in her cubicle behind a massive monitor. She ducked down even further to be sure they didn't see her. The topic they were laughing over was one she had strong feelings about. She guessed they'd never had their black hearts broken. Jerks.

"You won't believe this," her boss, Tom, said. "But I may know the perfect replacement for you. My assistant, Mallory. The girl's been engaged three times that I know of, and she still hasn't gotten married. She could not only give advice to your readers, but sympathy as well. The 'been there, done that,' kind."

"Oh, ho!" Brian said as both men chuckled.

That did it! She no longer could sit quietly by listening to them spew such garbage and laugh about her past. Fuming, she stood up. "Sympathy? You think I'd give them sympathy? Anyone who gets married these days is asking for trouble. It's a one-way ticket to misery and divorce."

"Speak of the devil," Tom said with a big grin, and not an

ounce of embarrassment over his words about her. "Brian, meet Mallory Conway. Mallory, this is Brian Abernathy, editor of the *Village Gazette*."

"The only devil around here is you, Tom Campilongo. Hello, Mr. Abernathy." She stuck out her hand to Abernathy. "Nice to meet you. And please ignore my boss's comments. He doesn't have a clue about people. Only real estate."

Abernathy gaped at her as they shook hands, then croaked, "Nice to meet you, too. And call me Brian, please."

Tom chuckled. "She is the most opinionated, and the best, assistant I've ever had. Seems like advice columnist material to me."

"Can you write?" Brian asked.

She was astonished that he would take her boss's comments seriously. "I have a degree in English, and I write puff-piece listings for homes all day long. So, yes, I can write. Especially fiction."

At those words, Brian's head had swiveled between her and Tom, as if he couldn't believe his good fortune. His face glowed. "With her background, it could be a completely different type of column. A 'misery loves company' column where people send in letters and emails, and Mallory could tell them that they don't know what *real* problems are, that she's been close three times but still hasn't gotten married!" Then, the man had the audacity to look at her and chuckle.

"Very funny." With a roll of her eyes at both men at this point, she plopped back down in her chair to go back to work. "You guys are such comedians."

"In fact, I like that name: 'Misery Loves Company,'" Brian added. "It's funny, sassy, and shows it would be an advice column with an edge."

Tom nodded. "Sounds good to me, too. And Mallory does write good listing copy, if that matters."

"For one thing," she added as she scooted her chair away

from the desk so that she could see them from the cubicle—and so that they could both see her scowl, "no one would want advice from a three-time loser. So right there, the column would be a dud."

"That's where you're wrong." Brian had moved toward her as he clasped his plump hands together. "They'd want to know your unique take on their situation for one thing, and the second reason is simply because 'misery loves company.' You'd make them realize that their problems aren't the end of the world."

Her mouth wrinkled. How could these two be so clueless? "People don't want to know that. They don't care about other's problems, just their own." She stopped talking as Brian stepped into the cubicle, tore a piece of paper from the notebook on her desk, wrote a number on it, and then folded it in half.

"I would need three columns per week," he said, handing her the paper and then stepping back from her. "Each would consist of one, sometimes two, readers' questions and your answers. Each column is short but pithy and thought-provoking. If you look at our 'Guidance from Gilda' column, you'll see it isn't very many words. I'll give you a couple of test questions, and if everything works out, *that* is your weekly pay."

She stood once more, all the while glowering at her boss. Tom had a grin on his face that told her he was finding all this beyond amusing. She opened the paper.

When she saw the number that Brian had written, her mouth dropped. "This is the amount I'd make each week just for writing three short columns filled with nothing but my opinions?" she asked.

He had nodded vigorously, which caused his jowls to quiver like pudding. "If the readers like what you have to say, and it is reflected in our advertising, it could go even higher."

Her breath had caught; her eyebrows high.. Then she had

relaxed her face and serenely smiled at both men. Dropping Brian's paper into her handbag, she asked, "When do I start?"

That was seven months ago.

Since then, "Misery Loves Company" had become so popular, it spread from the *Greenwich Village Gazette* to small advertising papers all over the tri-state area. With the now syndicated thrice-weekly, easy-to-write column, Mallory earned almost as much as she made working full time at Piaget.

With the two jobs, she was able to catch up on her credit card payments and might even be able to afford a somewhat decent apartment when the time came to give up her sublease.

Of course, no one except Brian, Tom, and a few other people with a "need to know" had any idea that Mallory Conway was the person behind the answers. All anyone else knew was that Dear Nellie dished out advice that was never sugar-coated and was often hard-to-take. But, ironically, most of the time, people wrote in to say it was spot on.

A few of her friends joked that "Nellie" was just like Mallory in that they'd both had multiple fiancés. She told them it only proved her situation wasn't as unique as they had tried to make it out to be.

Now, since Mallory had time before her date arrived, she opened up the "Dear Nellie" files on her computer. A letter caught her eye.

Dear Nellie,

I'm getting married in two months. Everyone tells me this is supposed to be the happiest time of my life, that I should enjoy all the things I need to do to plan for the wedding and the reception. Instead, I feel overwhelmed and frightened. My parents hired a wedding planner to help me, but now I feel as if it isn't my wedding, but hers. My fiancé says I'm just being silly, and that I really do want a big, beautiful wedding. But, in my heart, I don't. What's wrong with me? [Signed] Miserable to the Max

The letter hit close to home. Mallory didn't have to think twice about how to answer this one.

Continue with THIS CAN'T BE LOVE wherever fine books and ebooks are sold.

ABOUT THE AUTHOR

Joanne Pence was born and raised in northern California. She has been an award-winning, *USA Today* best-selling author of mysteries for many years, but she has also written historical fiction, contemporary romance, romantic suspense, a fantasy, and supernatural suspense. All of her books are now available as ebooks and in print, and most are also offered in special large print editions. Joanne hopes you'll enjoy her books, which present a variety of times, places, and reading experiences, from mysterious to thrilling, emotional to lightly humorous, as well as powerful tales of times long past.

Visit her at www.joannepence.com and be sure to sign up for Joanne's mailing list to hear about new books.